T reminded himself. *It all ends in a few months. Nothing here is permanent.*

"This is it," Candy began. "The moment we've been waiting for."

They paused in front of the door, Michael hesitant to spoil the drama of the moment by actually going into the house. Resisting the urge to pick Candy up and carry her, he put a hand at the small of her back and gently propelled her over the threshold.

The entry hall was gloomy and dark. He felt Candy shiver and put an arm around her. There were goose bumps on her arm. It would be folly to assume she was responding to his closeness, but it would be reassuring to know he wouldn't be the only one struggling through the next few months.

Dear Reader,

As Celebration 1000! moves into its third exciting month, Silhouette Romance is pleased to present a very special book from one of your all-time favorite authors, Debbie Macomber! In *The Bachelor Prince,* a handsome prince comes to America in search of a bride to save his country from ruin. But falling for the wrong woman made his duty a struggle. Was loving Hope Jordan worth losing his kingdom?

If you enjoyed Laurie Paige's WILD RIVER books in the Special Edition line, don't miss *A Rogue's Heart,* as Silhouette Romance carries on this series of rough-and-ready men and the women they love.

No celebration would be complete without a FABULOUS FATHER. This month, Gayle Kaye tells the heartwarming story of a five-year-old ballerina-in-the-making who brings her pretty dance teacher and her overprotective dad together for some very private lessons.

Get set for love—and laughter—in two wonderful new books: *Housemates* by Terry Essig and *The Reluctant Hero* by Sandra Paul. And be sure to look for debut author Robin Nicholas's emotional story of a woman who must choose between the man she loves and the town she longs to leave in *The Cowboy and His Lady.*

Next month, the celebration continues with books by beloved authors Annette Broadrick and Elizabeth August. Thanks so much for joining us during this very special event.

Happy reading!

Anne Canadeo
Senior Editor

Please address questions and book requests to:
Reader Service
U.S.: P.O. Box 1325, Buffalo, NY 14269
Canadian: P.O. Box 1050, Niagara Falls, Ont. L2E 7G7

HOUSEMATES
Terry Essig

Published by Silhouette Books
America's Publisher of Contemporary Romance

If you purchased this book without a cover you should be aware that this book is stolen property. It was reported as "unsold and destroyed" to the publisher, and neither the author nor the publisher has received any payment for this "stripped book."

For Bob.
It must be true love—we made it through the remodeling.

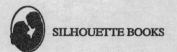 SILHOUETTE BOOKS

ISBN 0-373-19015-8

HOUSEMATES

Copyright © 1994 by Terry Parent Essig

All rights reserved. Except for use in any review, the reproduction or utilization of this work in whole or in part in any form by any electronic, mechanical or other means, now known or hereafter invented, including xerography, photocopying and recording, or in any information storage or retrieval system, is forbidden without the written permission of the editorial office, Silhouette Books, 300 East 42nd Street, New York, NY 10017 U.S.A.

All characters in this book have no existence outside the imagination of the author and have no relation whatsoever to anyone bearing the same name or names. They are not even distantly inspired by any individual known or unknown to the author, and all incidents are pure invention.

This edition published by arrangement with Harlequin Enterprises B.V.

® and TM are trademarks of Harlequin Enterprises B.V., used under license. Trademarks indicated with ® are registered in the United States Patent and Trademark Office, the Canadian Trade Marks Office and in other countries.

Printed in U.S.A.

Books by Terry Essig

Silhouette Romance

House Calls #552
The Wedding March #662
Fearless Father #725
Housemates #1015

Silhouette Special Edition

Father of the Brood #796

TERRY ESSIG

says that her writing is her escape valve from a life that leaves very little time for recreation or hobbies. With a husband and six young children, Terry works on her stories a little at a time, between seeing to her children's piano, sax and trombone lessons, their gymnastics, ice skating and swim team practices, and her own activities of leading a Brownie troop, participating in a car pool and attending organic chemistry classes. Her ideas, she says, come from her imagination and her life—neither one of which is lacking!

Reasons not to buy a house with Michael:

1. He doesn't know the first thing about decorating.
2. He wants to spend all our money on screwdrivers and wrenches.
3. All we do is argue.
4. He's too good-looking, too smart—too good to be true.

Reasons to buy a house with Michael:

1. I could teach him a lot about decorating.
2. He looks adorable in a tool belt.
3. We fight a lot, but making up with Michael is *so* much fun!
4. He's too good-looking, too smart—too good to pass up.

Chapter One

"He just makes me want to scream."

Candice Barr glared at the friend occupying the desk next to hers and tapped her pencil in an irritated fashion.

Giving an exaggerated sigh, Tina Hartnett reluctantly looked up from her calculations and said, "All right, I'll bite. Who makes you want to scream?"

Candy jerked her head in the direction of the two men emerging from her boss's private sanctuary. They were deeply involved in conversation. "Oh, come on. Him! Michael. Michael Cane. Don't try and tell me you haven't noticed that ever since he transferred here a couple of months ago he spends most of his time buttering up Bob."

Obligingly, Tina Hartnett squinted across the large, open, bullpen-style work space she and Candy shared with about thirty of Nelson Robotics' finest. "They look like they're talking business to me."

8   HOUSEMATES

"Oh, yeah, right. They're always together lately. How come none of the rest of us have that much business to discuss with Bob?"

"Probably because none of the rest of us have generated the amount of sales Michael has lately. You have to admit he's pulled off a couple of fairly amazing coups since he's been here. I heard he's about ready to close on another whopper deal that will put his sales total well over his quota for the year, and it's only August. Word is he's gunning for Golden Circle, not just hundred-percent club."

That bit of news took Candy back. "He's planning on selling five times his quota by the end of the year, not just a hundred percent? In this economy? That's ridiculous." The man was crazy. But she looked doubtfully at the receding backs of their suits as Bob and Michael moved together out of the area that housed Nelson's regular account executives.

"Know what I think?" Tina asked as she went back to studying her computer screen.

"What?"

"I think you're jealous." Tina punched a few keys on her board and watched the configuration on the screen adjust. "I think you're so used to being the up-and-coming fair-haired girl around here, it's killing you to see a newcomer do as well as Michael's doing."

"That's the dumbest thing I've ever heard," Candy rebutted irritably, her eyes narrowing as Michael and Bob disappeared from sight. "And besides, there's no cause for me to be jealous. After all, I've had a couple of decent sales this year myself." She dragged her eyes back to her screen and stared at the numbers in front of her. This particular account, however, was a thorn in her side. These

HOUSEMATES

were Robeson's Rust-safe figures. In three years, they'd yet to buy their first piece of anything from her. "I've sold seventy percent of my quota for the year already," she defended herself as she glowered at her screen.

"And you may very well make hundred-percent club, which this year is a weekend in Miami. But I know you. You're so darn competitive it'll kill you if Michael sells five times his yearly quota and makes Golden Circle. He'll get wined and dined by the company's top brass for a solid week in the Bahamas."

"I am not jealous," Candy said through gritted teeth.

Tina shrugged. "Fine, you're not jealous. Let's just say I find it odd that not another person in the office has a problem with him. Hard worker, decent guy—and not bad-looking, either. What more could you want? He's certainly better than that self-aggrandizing idiot he replaced."

"Not much," Candy groused. "The estimable Mr. Cane took over Ted Beaseley's lease when he moved out, did you know that? Beaseley lived in my building! I can't even get away from the man when I go home at night. And for your information, it just so happens—" She stopped herself in midsentence. "Never mind. Just forget it." She took a deep breath. "Are we still going to lunch at McDaniel's?"

"Yeah, sure, I could use the break, but I've got to straighten these figures out first. Give me forty-five minutes." Tina turned her attention back to her work. Candy tried to do the same. She'd been about to blurt that Michael was also forward and too cocksure. He'd asked her out during his first week here. Heck, it had only been the third day. Don't tell her Michael Cane wasn't a fast mover. Of course, she'd turned him down. But something told her Tina would think her silly for having done so, and Candy knew she wouldn't be able to explain her reasoning. She just didn't like him, and it wasn't jealousy, darn it.

She squirmed in her chair. Man, what was with her today? Usually she had no trouble focusing on her work. This was all Michael's fault. Something about him disturbed her, that's all there was to it. Well, she'd simply have to force herself to pay attention. Maybe she'd fake them all out and sell five times her quota and make Golden Circle herself. Ha! That would show them. Grimly, she perused the Robeson's Rust-safe figures.

"Now if Gary Felding were to drop off the end of the earth, even for a short time, I could make real progress here," she muttered disgruntledly to herself. Unfortunately, he was her contact at Robeson's. He was the kind whose necktie always matched the silk handkerchief in his jacket pocket. He even wore a diamond pinkie ring. His name was synonymous with slime-ball in Candy's dictionary. "His entire operation is so backward over there, it's pathetic." She snapped her fingers. "I know. He can go with Michael for a week in the Bahamas! I'll even pay his way." She'd get his place automated with some state-of-the-art robotics while he was gone and end up the office heroine.

Fat chance, she thought. Gary was playing a waiting game. In his view women were made for one purpose. He'd reluctantly agreed to do business with her months ago, but only if she provided her body as a thank-you. In his dreams! His antiquated service would rust itself motionless before that happened.

Besides, he had shifty eyes. She didn't know how his wife could stand living with a guy who couldn't look you in the face. You saw some men and you could just tell they were out for what they could get, Candy decided. Then there were others, like Michael, whose golden brown eyes

HOUSEMATES 11

held yours, like it or not. His eyes spoke of bedrock solidity and long-term commitment, neither of which she was interested in right then. Besides, he was pushy. And she could resist that kind of appeal, no problem. But when he'd approached her that first week she'd also seen a brief flare of what she suspected was usually a well-controlled and well-hidden sensuality. Just enough for the answering spark she felt to scare her, which was the real reason she'd turned down his request for a date. She intended to take her career very seriously for the present, until she was firmly established. Then she'd think about home and hearth. For now she had other priorities, and men like Michael who got in the way at work and threatened her peace of mind on other fronts were definitely to be avoided.

Tina interrupted her thoughts. "Candy..."

The sound of a voice so close to her side made Candy jump. "What?"

Tina gave her a curious look. "That's your phone. How about giving the rest of us a break and picking it up?"

"Oh, sure. Sorry." She reached for the buzzing instrument, her face red. "Hello?"

"Candy? Mary Frank here. How are you doing?"

Candy couldn't think of any logical explanation for what ailed her, so she took the easy way out. "Fine, Mary, everything's just fine. What's new with you? You find any more monstrosities masquerading as houses you want to drag me through?"

Candy could hear the excitement in her friendly neighborhood realtor's voice when she began to speak.

"I think I've found it," Mary announced. "I really think I have."

Candy sat up straight. "You have?" She was suddenly able to concentrate with no problem. "You've got a fixer-upper I can handle?"

"It just came over the wire for the multiple listings a couple of minutes ago," Mary confirmed. "Of course I haven't actually seen it, but from the description, I think we need to get out there. Tonight, if possible."

Candy tried to think what was on her calendar at home. "I think I can do that. It's that good, huh?"

"I'm fairly familiar with the section of town they're talking about. It's wonderful. Walking distance to stores, church, schools and the train downtown. The streets still have the original brick pavers and the trees are mature. Every one of them's a minimum of fifty or sixty years old, so there's plenty of shade."

"Sounds too good to be true."

"It may well be, but we'll never know unless we go check it out. I'll pick up a key and swing by your place around six-thirty."

"You're on."

"Man, this place is a dump," Candy whispered as she started down the stairs from the second floor of the house.

"That's the beauty of the place," Mary stated firmly. "Its structural integrity, terrific floor plan and generous room sizes are well camouflaged under a heavy coat of grime and gross decorating. Not many prospective buyers will be able to see past that."

Candy paused on the landing and eyed the light fixture growing out of the newel post. It—she—was Grecian, bare breasted and, in keeping with the surrounding walls and woodwork, gold. She had no lower body, the newel post took over at her waist. She held a shattered light bulb aloft

HOUSEMATES 13

in one hand. "I'm glad you explained that to me," was all Candy said.

Mary flicked a hand negligently at the listing Greek. "Cosmetics. Don't let yourself get sucked in by that. This can all be changed. If the place didn't need work, it wouldn't be a 'handyman's special' and they'd be asking top dollar. The trick is you've got to have vision, know what to jump at. All the fixing up in the world would be wasted on something structurally unsound. Obviously the house has been vandalized, so it doesn't look great. But this place is solid as a rock. I can feel it. It could be a gem."

Frankly, Candy thought, the place gave her the heebie-jeebies. It reeked of almost a century of families. It cried out for children to fill it up, and she had none, wanted none for several more years. This wasn't for her. She glanced around one more time and began justifying her first response, which had been to walk right back out the front door and never look back.

"I don't know about the solid part, Mary. I know I told you I wanted a fixer-upper, but this goes beyond mere fixing up. This is rehabber hell. The whole roof is bad. Didn't you see the watermarks on the ceiling in three of the four bedrooms up there? There's only one bath, and it's up there, too. Did you see that extremely ominous bulge in its ceiling? It hangs down a good foot or more. Probably full of water from the leaky roof. It wouldn't surprise me if not only the roof needed replacing, but the boards underneath, as well."

Candy left the Grecian goddess behind and continued down the stairs. "And the kitchen needs to be torched. It's got leftover linoleum from the floor masquerading as a countertop. There are ninety-year-old, obviously home-made cupboards posing as cabinets. The stove is one step down the evolutionary line from a wood-burner, and if the refrigerator didn't have an electric cord on it, you'd swear it was an icebox. Kitchens are *expensive* to redo."

Mary remained unfazed. "The roof is nothing. There are no water stains in the basement, which is way more important, and the floors and stairs are level. The walls look plumb, too. I'm telling you, with a little love, care and a lot of elbow grease, this would be wonderful. A real family kind of house, you know?"

"I'm glad you realize that. You may have noticed I don't have a family. What am I going to do with a house this size? It's not a starter house. And I could never get through all this work by myself. Good grief, the back porch is hanging on to the house by force of habit, the boiler is turn-of-the-century, and have you checked out the walls and ceilings?" Candy pirouetted, pointing as she did so. "They're all gold. The woodwork, even the radiators have been gilded. God only knows how many coats of primer it would take to cover that."

"Listen, kiddo," Mary said, "I know the real-estate agent who's got the listing for this place. He has the same problem you're having tonight. No vision. Can't see past cosmetics. Added to that, his office is a couple of suburbs away where prices are generally lower, anyway. I don't know how he got the listing but, sweetie, the asking price he put on this place is giving it away. I'm telling you, not as your friend but as a professional realtor, this is the one to go for." She slapped the listing in her hand for emphasis. "I mean it, this is it."

Candy had almost reached the front door. Pausing, she glanced around uncertainly. "You really think so?" she asked. "I was thinking of a little bungalow. Something I could handle with a coat of fresh paint and new drapes." She sounded almost wistful.

"No pain, no gain," Mary grunted.

HOUSEMATES

Candy felt cornered. "You said it yourself. This is a family kind of house. It's much too large for me. What would I do with four bedrooms?"

"Get married and fill them?"

"No. Seriously, I—"

Mary was losing patience. "Oh, come on, Candy. Think about it! The potential of this place is so much greater than anything else we've seen. View it as the means to an end, instead of the end, if you have to. You could make enough profit on this place fixing it up and selling it to a young family—did I tell you the school district here is superior?—that you could put thirty or forty percent down on a smaller place, instead of the ten percent you're planning on."

Candy thought about that. She could, couldn't she? Make a killing on this one, then pay cash for the little bungalow of her dreams. Hmm. She reached for the front doorknob only to have it turn under her hand. She stared at it while taking a step back. Lord, the place was haunted by the ghost of families past. "Someone's here," she whispered to Mary. "They're coming in. What'll we do?" The door swung open, revealing two solid male forms. Burglars?

No such luck. One of them looked annoyingly familiar.

"Hi, Jack," Mary said while Candy tried to calm her heart by patting her chest. "Showing a client through?"

Jack smiled and nodded. "You know how it is, no rest for the wicked."

"Well, we're all done, so we'll just get out of your—"

"Hello, Candy."

"Michael." Candy nodded her recognition and avoided his gaze by looking down at the floor. The man was like a sticker burr. There was no getting rid of him. Then again, when she looked at a sticker burr, all she saw was a sticker

16 HOUSEMATES

burr. Somebody else had pulled one off the seat of his pants and made a fortune inventing Velcro. Vision, that was the thing. She finally stopped staring at his running shoes and actually looked at him. Her eyes widened. Either her pique with the coups he'd pulled at the office had blinded her, or Michael was one of those guys who simply didn't wear suits well. She dropped her gaze again, then forced it back up. Now jeans he wore well. *Very* well. His hips were slimmer than she'd have guessed, his chest broader. "Holy cow," she said under her breath.

"What?" Mary asked.

"Nothing," Candy muttered. Look at that man, she thought. Now that his neck was released from the confines of a tie, and the collar of his soft cotton shirt lay open, short brown hair curled into view. Just enough to spell out MALE BODY in capital letters. Just enough to make her hand itch to undo the next button and check out what lay below.

Shocked to her toes by the errant path her mind was taking, she raised her eyes to his face. For the first time, she realized his hair, a warm golden brown, matched his eyes. And the man was definitely handsome. Not magazine handsome, but his features had a masculine appeal she suddenly found very...appealing as the dusky light played over his features. If he stretched, she still doubted he'd make six feet—which was actually rather nice. Being towered over got tiring after a while.

It must be seeing him out of context that was throwing her, she decided. But whatever it was, it had to stop. She'd seen this house first, and this was one sale he was not going to get. Still, when his lips moved she had to force her brain to focus on the words they formed.

"I didn't know you were thinking of buying a house."

There was a lot he didn't know about her, and she intended to keep it that way. The man was dangerous to her peace of mind. And here he was again, acting ever so polite while he plotted to steal *her* house.

"Oh, I've been looking for quite some time now." She hoped to discourage him. Suddenly she wanted this place more than anything else she could think of. "I'm afraid this one's really a wreck, though. Unless, of course, you're a rehabber on the side?" He couldn't be. He spent all his time closing giant sales and discussing them with Bob.

"Not in the traditional sense, although several friends of mine have made a peck of money rehabbing beauties like this one and selling at a handsome profit. All I want to do is break into the market, not make a habit of it. Prices are so much higher here than where I came from that I'm afraid a fixer-upper is the only way in."

"Yes," Candy said reluctantly. She was hesitant to agree with anything Michael said, she realized. It seemed dangerous somehow. "Rent is a waste of money. At least with a mortgage, there's an end in sight and you own something when you get through."

There seemed to be nothing else to say. They stood staring at each other. Because Candy was inside while Michael stood a step down on the outside, they were eye to eye. Michael tucked his hands into his back pockets and rocked for a moment. "So," he finally said. "I take it you're not interested?"

"I didn't say that," she said hastily.

"You are interested?"

Why did he have to keep pushing? "I'm not sure," she said.

"Uh-huh. Well, you won't mind if we look around, then."

18   HOUSEMATES

Candy realized she was blocking the doorway. She was suddenly feeling protective of the old heap. "Surely you're not interested in something this run-down?"

Michael studied the gloom behind her thoughtfully. "Of course I haven't been inside yet, but the exterior appears rather intriguing."

"You're kidding." If Michael had the vision thing on top of everything else, she'd just spit.

"Here. Come and I'll show you."

And he touched her. He reached out and took her arm. She wanted to resist but, instead, almost fell out the door and into his arms. Her whole arm tingled, for crying out loud.

Michael appeared to notice nothing untoward as he tugged her along the front of the house pointing out interesting architectural features that Candy hadn't even noticed. Mary stayed behind to speak to Michael's realtor, who was obviously a business acquaintance.

"Look at these three sets of double-arched French doors," Michael directed. "They're beautifully spaced across the front of the house. From what I can tell they all open from the living room, which means for a party this whole patio out here could be used for overflow."

A child's birthday party, Candy thought. Balloons tied to the knobs of the open French doors. "But the patio concrete is all cracked and heaved up around the tree roots," she protested.

"Certainly whoever buys the place would have to dig it out and repour it," Michael admitted. "If it were me, I'd change the shape, though. Something curved and amorphic, instead of rectangular, don't you think?"

"I hadn't given it much thought," she admitted weakly. Darn it, anyway, he did have vision—the kind Mary had spent the past hour harping about.

HOUSEMATES 19

"Isn't it great the way the garage is connected to the house by way of this swooping stucco wall? And I love how the old-fashioned gateway to the backyard is cut right through it. Gives the place a sort of Spanish feel. Even has ivy growing on it," he noted with satisfaction as they stood in the driveway.

"Well, I suppose if you patched the stucco..."

"Yeah, you'd have to work your butt off on this place, that's for sure, but the potential is here."

Then he really annoyed her by taking out a notebook and making a bunch of notations in it. Darn his rotten hide. She'd seen this place first! "Michael, this house is too big for you. It's a family kind of house, you know what I mean? It needs a bathroom tucked into the first floor someplace, but other than that, it's perfect. Four nice-sized bedrooms, fenced in yard, a park just down the block. What more could a family ask? You couldn't possibly use this much space."

"No, I don't need it, but I'm not sure I want to pass it up, either." He rocked on his heels. "If the inside's not too bad, it might be the kind of thing you could work on through the fall and winter, dump onto the spring hot market and walk away with a small bundle. Enough to put down a fat deposit on a nice condo downtown." He shrugged. "Then again, maybe I'd just keep it. You don't have to need a nice big place to appreciate it."

Candy began edging away from him. His thinking was totally misguided, she knew it. This house was turn-of-the-century. It stunk to high heaven of generations of families being brought up there. The last one through had let it get run-down, but anyone staying in the place too long would have the familial instinct rub off on them, she was sure.

Then again, what was she worried about? If she bought it, she'd only own it long enough to fix up and sell for a quick profit. She'd be safely in her little bungalow before she knew it. Besides, if she didn't buy it, Michael might get it, and she couldn't stand the thought of letting that happen without a fight.

Mary came around the corner of the house. "You ready to go?" she asked.

Candy paused, unsure. Leaving *her* house unprotected and unguarded with Michael on the loose didn't seem smart. Still, what could she do? It would be dark soon. "Yeah, sure. I guess."

"Did you want to see the backyard? It's a little overgrown right now, but I think it would shape up nicely."

"No, that's okay. You can tell me about it in the car." Candy grabbed her realtor's arm and began steering her down the driveway. She needed to get away from *him*. Needed to think. The house would have to fend for itself the next few hours. Actually, it looked as if it had been doing that for quite some time. "See you, Michael."

Michael responded absently. When Candy looked back over her shoulder, he was making more notes in that infernal little book of his.

A car pulled into the spot behind Mary's. A young woman about Candy's age, she estimated, got out with a professional-looking type carrying a briefcase. Another car drove slowly down the brick-paved street, its occupants craning their necks as they checked out the house with the For Sale sign.

"It's going to go fast," Mary commented, slipping into the driver's seat.

"All right, all right. Let's go back to the office and talk," Candy replied irritably as she got into the car.

"And look. There's your friend, Michael. He and Jack must be checking out the master bedroom."

HOUSEMATES
21

"I said all right, didn't I?" Candy responded, her tone a bit surly as she twisted her head to look back as Mary drove away. Michael was perfectly framed in the master-bedroom window. "His vision's not *that* good, you know. He wears glasses at work."

"You're being petty, you know, and I bet he looks cute in glasses. He looks pretty darn good without them, I know that much. One of those men made for jeans, I think." Mary sighed. "Be that as it may, I want to underline that that place could be a gold mine. In this kind of neighborhood, whatever you sank into the house you'd get back tripled. But you need to jump fast on it, if you're going to jump at all."

"I know, I know."

Two days later Candy was still fuming. She'd succumbed to Mary's logic only to discover that what Mary thought was a steal was out of Candy's league. She'd spent the last forty-eight hours being as creative as possible in thinking up ways to finance it. There was just no way. No matter how she finagled, the funds simply weren't there. Not only that, there was just no way she could remodel that massive wreck on her own. She didn't have the pure physical strength some of the tasks would require.

"So, are you putting a bid in on that house we saw, Candy?"

She glanced up from the file she'd been staring at. *He* was at her desk. "Michael!" she exclaimed.

"Yes, Michael. Are you?" he persisted, looking down at her.

Candy swiveled slightly in her chair. What was it about him that made her so aware of him as a man? Especially when she didn't want to be. It was discouraging.

22 HOUSEMATES

She doubted they had much in common. She enjoyed forgetting work after hours and going out with a group of friends to relax.

Her computer screen was reflected in his glasses. She could no more picture him nightclubbing or turning into a party animal than she could see her mother agreeing it had been a good idea for her to move out and into her own apartment.

Maybe his very solidity contributed to the uneasiness she felt around him. Other men, just as nice looking—some better, in fact, than Michael—were easy to ignore. Michael, especially with all those columns of numbers where his eyes should be, had an aura of solid intelligence. You could trust the advice of a man whose eyes mirrored rows of numerical data. Trust she could understand. It was her awareness of him as a man that drove her crazy.

"After doing some figuring and making some calls, it seems I'm pretty much out of the picture," she replied. "When I started looking, I was thinking of something smaller. I can't scrape together the financing for this one, no matter how great a deal it is. How about you? You going to put in a bid?"

"I've made a few phone calls myself," Michael admitted. "Basically, I'm too conservative to go that far out on a limb alone, and if I take on a partner, then the house wouldn't be mine. You know what I mean?"

He'd put his hand on the back of her chair and leaned closer to her when he'd spoken. Now he was at the wrong angle for his glasses to reflect the numbers from her screen. She felt a rush of panic. His eyes held hers. Warm and brown with small gold flecks floating in their liquid depths. He no longer appeared the financial wizard. Rather, she was frightened the way a woman is when she knows her life is about to change and there isn't a damn thing she can do about it. His breath feathered her hair. She closed her eyes in an effort to concentrate, but with the removal of visual interference, her awareness of his closeness intensified.

Feeling a bit desperate, she opened them again. "A partner? I hadn't thought of that." It could work. Unfortunately the only other person she knew who was interested in a rehab project was Michael, and that was out of the question. She'd call around after work. Beat the bushes a bit. "But you're right. It wouldn't be really yours, then, would it?"

Michael spoke slowly. "No. Still, if it's the only possibility, maybe I could make arrangements to buy them out after a certain number of years or something. I don't know. I'm still thinking about it." He stood looking down at her, eyeing her screen. There was no way to hide the data displayed there. "So. Got any interesting sales on the horizon?"

She'd die before she admitted she'd hit dead ends with her last few sales calls. "Oh, there are always possibilities. How about you?"

He shrugged nonchalantly. "As you say. Lots of possibilities out there."

"Yes, and I need to get back to them. So if you'll excuse me?" She smiled ever so politely, then paused. Might as well be as negative as possible. "Too bad about the house, though. I mean, there's really no time to iron out the details of a partnership, is there? It would all have to be down in black and white, and Mary, my realtor, says action on the house is heating up. Lots of people going through."

Thoughtfully, she shuffled a stack of papers into their folder. "A partnership would really be difficult. How could you possibly decide whether or not you could work with another person in that kind of stressful situation and set up a game plan in a couple of days or less? Things could end up a mess. I mean, you never really know somebody until you're working practically on top of him—or her—day in and day out." She blushed, wondering if Michael's mind had taken her unthinking remark about being on top of another person and run with it the way hers had.

It was hard to tell. Michael appeared contemplative. "True," he allowed at last. "But as you say, not much time to work anything out, is there? Well, I'll see you later, I guess. I'm late for an appointment at Lorenzo's."

"That's the third call your team has made there this week," she remembered. "Is anything happening?"

"Nothing solid yet. He's being a reluctant sell, but I'll get him."

"What are you trying to sell the poor guy? He just updated every robotic on his assembly line last year. They couldn't have recouped the original investment cost in increased productivity yet, and you're already trying to upgrade him?"

"I believe I did indicate he was being a reluctant sell."

Candy had been balancing on the back two legs of her chair. The front coasters hit the carpet with a dull thump when Michael stretched before her and slipped on the suit coat he'd been carrying over his solid, broad shoulders.

"But," Michael continued. "If I'm going to make Golden Circle again this year, I'm going to have to sell something to somebody. Actually a lot of somebodies. Lorenzo's is as good a place to start as any."

Did he say make Golden Circle *again?* He'd done it before? Her eyes narrowed and she turned back to her screen. "You sure a week in the Bahamas is worth all this?"

"I need the commissions. Maybe next time a house like that comes on the market I'll be able to do something about it."

"Yeah," Candy agreed dispiritedly. Provided there was a next time.

Chapter Two

The very next evening, after a voice-mail message from Michael and a rather badgering phone call from Mary Frank, Candy found herself sitting in a deli across a small table from her office nemesis. She eyed him warily, knowing what was coming. Mary had made it clear that Michael had received a similar phone call from her realtor friend, Jack.

They were here to discuss the possibility of combining their resources to buy the house and fix it up in time for the spring market, with each walking away with enough profit to afford whatever living accommodations they chose. Logically, it made perfect sense. Unfortunately Candy wasn't operating logically at the moment.

She felt like a fly being beckoned into a spider's web. Panic had risen to about throat level. She swallowed and gave Michael what she hoped passed for a game smile as she reminded herself what she knew of spiderwebs. Arachnids made only the horizontally spun threads sticky.

HOUSEMATES

They walked on the vertical supports, which kept them from getting ensnared in their own webs. If spiders could tread in the face of danger, so could she. She'd simply have to be cautious. Very cautious. Michael was not getting even half that house without her.

She wished Mary had never even taken her to see the place. She just knew a partnership with Michael was going to be a nightmare. She tried to buoy herself with the thought that just because she found Michael inexplicably attractive—even though he was all wrong for her—didn't mean he was suffering a similar malady. Unfortunately she knew with the innate knowledge that had served women down through the ages that he *was* interested. Hadn't he asked her out three days after his arrival in the office?

"Any luck at Lorenzo's?" she inquired. Anything to break the silence.

He shrugged. "They still need a bit of convincing."

"Oh. Too bad." She shot a falsely sympathetic smile across the table. "I may have something starting to heat up at a rustproofing account I've got. They're ripe for updating." Ha! In her dreams. She willed herself to forget about the length of male thigh currently forced to rest right up against hers by the shallow depth of the table. The weight of his summer-business-suit pant leg was not enough, even when combined with her nylons and silky skirt, to negate the feel of solid masculine leg plastered up against her. The warmth he emanated practically singed her panty hose. Oddly, she shivered.

"Cold?"

She couldn't help it. She shivered again and was disgusted with herself. The after-work crowd was so heavy in the small deli, that blaming the air-conditioning certainly wouldn't work. There was no way he'd believe she was anything but overheated. She smiled sickly. "Maybe I'm

28   HOUSEMATES

coming down with the cold that's going around the office."

He looked doubtful. "I didn't know there was a bug going around."

"Well, there is," she stated defiantly. "There definitely is. Now, could we please get down to business?"

Michael put his hands up in surrender. "Okay, okay. No need to get testy." Then he pulled out a notebook and began quoting from a hodgepodge of housing-repair estimates mixed in with mortgage rates and a study of neighborhood demographics. God only knew where he'd dug all that up. When he finally wound down, he set the notebook aside and took a sip of his light beer. "In all honesty, I think Jack and your friend Mary just want their commission out of us, even if they have to split it. But I've come to the conclusion that their idea of the two of us combining our resources, since neither one of us can afford it on our own, is solid. I believe the investment would be sound and produce a good yield. Of course, I'll still want our individual responsibilities spelled out in black and white and we'll have to agree on some rules for getting along so this thing doesn't degenerate into a free-for-all. Also, we need a home inspection," he informed her. "There are plenty of things we may have missed here. We need the radon levels checked, for example, and—"

"The thing is," Candy interrupted thoughtfully, "Mary called again just as I was getting ready to come meet you. She wanted me to know there were four showings again yesterday and a couple more scheduled for this evening. She says the average is twenty-three showings before a bid comes in. The house is almost at that level now."

Michael tapped his pencil on the table. "In other words, if we don't move we might lose it?"

HOUSEMATES

"That's what she says."

He dragged a corn chip through a mound of guacamole and munched it thoughtfully. "I don't know. I hate going into something without knowing all the facts and figures."

Candy hated going into anything at all with Michael. She leaned back in her chair and took a contemplative sip of her wine cooler. She and Tina had thoroughly discussed her options after Mary's phone call.

Tina had been her typical tactful self, Candy remembered.

"What, are you out of your mind?" her friend had yelped. "This is only the perfect solution to all your problems. I can't see why you're dithering."

Candy had sighed and glanced sideways at Tina. "I can't explain it. It's irrational."

"What's irrational?"

"It's just that something like remodeling a home with somebody is pretty intimate. I mean, for all practical purposes, you might as well be married to the guy for however long it takes."

Tina called up a file on her computer and while she waited for it to appear on the screen, said, "Listen, I know your mother has counseled you since you were in diapers not to get married too young. You told me all about how you were supposed to learn from her mistake. But for crying out loud, this isn't a real marriage. It's only a temporary arrangement. And even if you *were* getting married, you're twenty-four, not seventeen the way she was. You've got job skills. You wouldn't have to wait tables to support your family if push came to shove."

Candy shoved a disk into her drive and frowned as figures appeared on the screen. "I told you it was irrational.

Anyway, I know there's no chance of anything *personal* developing with Michael Cane. For one thing, I'm too sensitive about my name to let it."

"What's your name got to do with anything?"

"Tina, you *know* how I feel about my name. I *hate* being called Candy Barr. Changing it when I got married is my out, and I intend to use it."

"So use it," Tina counseled. "I fail to see— Ohh. From the frying pan into the fire, huh? You'd be Candy Cane." She laughed.

"See what I mean? The thought of marrying Michael is a little hard to take seriously. Kind of like a bad joke." Candy started laughing, too. "See? I can't help it. And if you think about it, it's not funny. Not really."

Tina scrolled down on her screen. "Picture this," she said with a smirk that boded no good. "A December wedding. The bridesmaids would be done up in diagonally striped red-and-white sheaths. It would be so—"

"If you say cute, you'd better be prepared to die."

Tina sobered. "Okay, okay. Listen, I know a guy with some extra cash who might be willing to go in for a percentage of the profits if you just can't deal with Michael."

Candy perked up. "Oh, yeah? What's his name?"

"Steven Land."

Candy's screen blipped dark as its protective device kicked in the way it did when nothing had been entered for a while. It matched the look she shot Tina. "Very funny. I'd probably be sued for copyright infringement. Candy Land. Good grief."

Her coworker had gone off into gales of laughter to which Candy had responded, "Oh, shut up. I've got work to do."

HOUSEMATES 31

"Candy!" A very male voice startled her out of her thoughts.

She focused her eyes and was startled to find herself back in the deli with Michael across from her, rather than Tina. "What! I mean, what?"

He sighed. "Have you heard anything I've said at all?"

Candy straightened and took a sip of her cooler, although alcohol would do little to clear her head, she supposed. "Sure I did. Uh, what came after you said you wanted the radon checked?"

He stared at her. "Candy, that was five minutes ago, at least. Where in the world did you go?"

The last thing she wanted to go into was an explanation of the conversation she'd had with Tina. Men were touchy about discussions of marriage, particularly when you'd yet to even have a first date. He'd think her more than a tad presumptuous. "It's been a long day," she improvised. "I wasn't thinking about anything in particular. My mind was just sort of drifting." Yeah, and into very dangerous territory. "I'm exhausted. Let's call it a night," she suggested as she leaned over to snag her purse from the floor at her feet. She paused, her hand on the strap. She contemplated Michael while she chewed off her lipstick. "We've got to make a decision, though, first, don't we? Let's go for it," she finally said, for the first time understanding how David Farragut felt sailing into Mobile Bay, yelling, "Damn the torpedoes, full speed ahead." He'd pulled it off; so could she. She wanted that house. She was going to have it. She laughed at danger. Ha! This was business and she'd darn well keep it that way. "I'll call Mary first thing in the morning, all right?"

Michael studied the militant gleam in her eye for a moment, then agreed. "Okay, fine. Let's do it."

32   HOUSEMATES

*   *   *

Candy had several messages on her answering machine when she got home. Only one got her adrenaline pumping, however.

"Hello, Candy? This is Mary. Listen, I've just heard from the realtor who's listing that house you're interested in. Another agent called and is on her way over with a bid. He's assuming a twenty-four-hour acceptance window. He's had feelers from a couple of other agents, as well. It's decision time, kiddo. Give me a call when you check your phone mail. I'm in the office until around eight. After that, you can reach me at home. Oh, it's...almost seven o'clock right now."

Candy picked up the phone and punched in Michael's number. After several rings, his machine picked up. "Michael, this is Candy. Where'd you go? I figured you'd be too exhausted after badgering Lorenzo's all day to do anything but go straight home. Anyway, Mary called and time just ran out. We've either got to put in a bid now or forget the whole thing. My advice is not to worry about the radon. We're only going to be there a few months. Let the next people in worry about it. Call me." She left her number.

Candy's next call to her realtor was just as frustrating. "Mary? It's Candy. Where are you? You said you'd be there. Listen, I can't seem to get in touch with Michael, but I left a message on his machine. You better be right about this place's potential, lady. We're flying blind and taking your word for an awful lot. Get a bid ready, I guess. We'll let you know what numbers to fill in after Michael calls me back."

After a nerve-racking hour the phone finally rang. "Candy, hi."

HOUSEMATES

"Michael! I can't believe it's really you. I've done nothing but talk to machines since I got home. Where the heck did you disappear to?"

"Candy—"

"Where's your apartment? I know you're in this building someplace. Time's ticking away and—"

"Candy—"

"Just because the bid is good for twenty-four hours doesn't mean the sellers will take that full amount of time to make up their minds. I mean, they could be picking up the phone to accept it right this minute. They could—"

"You just let me know when it's my turn to talk, okay? I can wait."

"Oh, shut up. This is important. We've got to get back to Mary right away." Candy wrapped the telephone cord around her wrist and wished it was Michael's neck. Couldn't he understand they were about to lose their house?

His voice sounded smug as it came back over the wire. "Candy, I know all about the other bids. I've just been with Jack."

Candy clutched at the phone and sank into the wing chair beside the living-room phone table. "What'd he say? Have they accepted the other bid? Is the house sold already?"

"Not quite."

"What the heck does that mean? How can a house be 'not quite' sold? Either it is or it isn't. That's like being a little bit pregnant. Not bloody likely." The words were no sooner out of her mouth when Candy flushed and wished desperately she could call them back. This was a big part of why Michael made her nervous. Ever since he'd shown up, references to marriage, pregnancy and babies were

34 HOUSEMATES

popping into her subconscious and out of her mouth. It had to stop.

"...so I told him I'd talk to you tonight and get back to him in the morning."

Candy shook the cobwebs out of her brain. "I'm sorry, Michael, what did you say?"

That now familiar gusty sigh came over the wire. "Okay, what's the last thing you heard me say?"

"Um, let me think. You'd talked to Jack what's-his-name."

"Good grief. Do you tune everybody out after their first sentence or two, or is the pleasure of repeating myself reserved strictly for me?"

"Well—"

"Never mind, I don't think I want to hear the answer. Rather than go through it all over again, here it is in a capsule. Two more agents have submitted bids from their clients. The seller knows that one from us may be in the offing, and maybe one or two others. They've decided to accept bids until three o'clock tomorrow afternoon, then cut it off. They'll choose the best offer from that pile and be done with it."

"This is becoming complicated."

"Anything worth having is."

Candy thought for a moment. "Can we find out what the other bids are so we can figure out if we want to top them or not?"

"No. They can't divulge the terms of the other offers. It's up to us to make an educated guess."

She tapped her toe impatiently, irritated with life as she lived it. Here she'd finally made a decision, and it could very well be all for naught. "Well, this certainly stinks."

HOUSEMATES

"I know it's late and you're tired, but I thought I'd come by with my notes and we could hash this thing out." He let the offer dangle.

Candy did not want the man in her apartment. It was too intimate, somehow, but there seemed very little choice in the matter. They had to finalize things. "Okay, Michael. Let's get this over with. I'm on the third floor in the northeast corner."

"I know. As soon as I've changed my pants and chucked my tie, I'll be there."

No, no! she wanted to scream. *Keep your suit on.* The key to success here was to remember this was a business deal, and the sight of Michael dressed casually in jeans and a T-shirt would make it harder for her to remember that.

Maybe she should put a skirt on. Something like what she'd wear to work. A silky blouse with one of those businesslike floppy bows right under your chin. She thought about that. The teal-blue one was clean and hanging in her closet, as she recalled.

Hosiery, she thought as she moved down the short hall. Yes, that would be good. With heels. Heels spoke of formality. Certainly much more so than the fuzzy mules her feet currently sported.

She'd just pulled off her loose T-shirt when the doorbell rang. Swearing, she slipped it back on. How the devil had Michael changed that fast when she hadn't even decided on the color shoe she wanted? She left her mules on and scuffed her way to the door, already annoyed.

She felt at even more of a disadvantage once she let him in. A business suit really did not do justice to Michael. Some men were like that. Jeans, on the other hand, did a great deal for him. He looked sexy as hell in denim that hugged his butt. He wore a brilliant aqua sweatshirt with the blatantly male jeans. The sleeves were pushed up to his elbows, displaying muscular forearms dusted with crisply curling brown hair. Candy found herself staring at them.

She shook her head to clear the image of those arms wrapped around her and took a breath. "Uh, have a seat, Michael."

He gave the furniture in the living room a quick glance and chose the sofa. Candy went for the wing chair opposite before grudgingly remembering her manners. "Did you have time for any dinner?" she asked. All she'd seen him eat that night was the guacamole appetizer.

"No," he admitted as he shuffled papers and dealt them out onto the coffee table. "I don't suppose you've got a couple of hot dogs you could throw my way out of the goodness of your heart?"

Goodness had little to do with it. She needed to keep her hands occupied while Michael was around. Stay busy so she would stop *noticing* things about him.

She jumped back up out of the chair and headed for the kitchen. "I'm sure I can come up with something. I haven't eaten yet, either." This was great. They'd *both* keep their hands busy. Hard to get into trouble that way.

When she came back with a tray of cut-up apples, vegetable spears, cheese chunks and a small loaf of French bread, Michael murmured, "Thanks," without looking up from the paper he was studying. Absently he patted the spot on the sofa next to him. "Here, sit here, so we can both see these numbers."

She knew it was a mistake, but he appeared studious and unthreatening as he peered through his glasses and squinted as he tried to decipher his own handwriting. She sat. And it was a mistake. She was immediately too warm, and it had nothing to do with it being the tail end of August.

HOUSEMATES

"Okay," she said, slightly panicked at her body's quick reaction to his nearness. She picked up an apple wedge, slapped a hunk of cheese on it and prepared to shove it into her mouth. "What did you want to show me?" Then she bit and kept occupied chewing.

"We need to decide all over again if we really want to do this," Michael began and picked up a carrot stick.

Candy gulped. Yes. Yes, they did. Only she was thinking more of Michael than the house.

Michael gestured with his carrot at the paper he was holding. "The problem we'll be running into is that these repair prices I've listed are little better than guesses on Jack's and my part. Unfortunately there's no time to have a home inspector come through now."

Candy sliced two pieces of bread from the loaf and handed one to Michael. "Couldn't we put in some kind of backup clause along the lines of the whole thing being null and void if the place can't pass a home inspection?"

Michael bit into the bread with strong white teeth Candy had never noticed before. This just kept getting worse and worse. She'd realized at the office he was a threat to her peace of mind. But here in her apartment, in those jeans— Oh, man, she was in trouble.

He answered her question thoughtfully. "We could, if we're not really sure how badly we want the house."

"What do you mean?"

He shrugged. "Apparently there'll be no haggling tomorrow. They'll take the most attractive bid and be done with it. It's an estate sale, and evidently the heirs are all out of state. They just want their money. Say we offer a little more money than somebody else, but we're loaded up with contingencies. Who do you think they'll choose?"

38 HOUSEMATES

Candy chewed her lip, instead of her French bread. "I see what you mean. They'd probably take the one that's free and clear."

Michael nodded in agreement. "That's the way I see it. If we're serious about this, we're going to have to go in with a completely clean offer for as much money as we can afford. When one shot is all you get, it'd better be your best."

She knew that. She understood the business world. She was a businesswoman, after all.

"There won't be any guarantees, nobody but us to go back and blame if it all blows up in our faces."

Crinkling her nose, Candy decided his alliteration left a bit to be desired. Maybe they should at least get the boiler checked first. No, she wanted that house, and that was that. If she had to live on antacids for the next six months, so be it. She set her bread down, wishing she had an antacid right then, sure she'd make herself sick if she attempted to eat another bite. God, she was a wreck. She looked from Michael to the picture of the house on their copy of the real-estate listing and back to Michael.

He leaned tiredly against the sofa back. His fingers had slipped under his glasses frames to rub his closed eyes. Why was she hesitating? She could handle a decaying house and a handsome salesman with one hand tied behind her back. She was woman! She was strong! She leaned forward and spoke intently, "Okay, Michael, what do you suggest for our offer?"

Chapter Three

Michael and Candy took the next morning off. Jack joined them in Mary Frank's office. The foursome spent the time trying to put together an attractive offer both Michael and Candy felt comfortable with. It was impossible. They settled for fairly attractive, extremely uncomfortable.

"I feel like a fool," Michael announced as he escorted Candy from Mary's office.

"How come?"

"You're supposed to haggle when you buy a house. It's an unwritten law. We're probably the first people in history to offer more than the asking price."

"It's only a thousand dollars more," Candy consoled.

"We didn't even ask to get the damage the vandals did cleaned up," he groused. Michael was wasting no time. No point in waiting around for buyer's remorse to strike. *Pre*buyer's remorse ate away at his state of mind like the moth that had gotten into his wool suits a year ago this summer. Intellectually he knew this was the right thing to do, but he was conservative by nature and his emotions had declared themselves in a state of disaster. Being with Candy didn't help. His peace of mind had gone on vacation the moment he'd met her and had yet to return. He should not be doing this.

"We didn't really have much of a choice," Candy defended. "Not if we truly want the place. But I know what you mean—I feel like I have 'sucker' written across my forehead. If anybody wanted to take a lick right now, I'd probably taste like sticky sweet cherry or orange dumdum."

Michael was willing to volunteer, he decided as he looked her over. Candy was living up to her name and definitely appeared good enough to eat. He put her into the passenger side of the car, jumped into the driver's seat and began driving before the temptation became too strong. When he got back to the office, he managed to lose himself in his work for the afternoon. But at his apartment that evening, he found himself pacing the floor. Finally he went and changed into running shorts and a T-shirt.

The run became longer than he'd anticipated. Their prospective house called him down streets only recently familiar until he stood in front of it gasping for air. He stared at the place.

Damn. He'd always talked a good line about wanting to get into real estate, but in reality, he was too fiscally conservative—cheap, his sister would have said. To get involved in something like this, well, his mind was obviously fried.

The whole mess was Jack's fault. Michael would have done well to remember that friendships suffer any time money's on the line. Jack had aligned himself with Can-

HOUSEMATES

dy's realtor against him. The two of them would laugh their way to the bank while Michael was left stuck with Candy resurrecting this place. Oh, God, did she even know anything about rehabbing? She was so gorgeous, was it even important? If he wasn't careful, he'd spend the fall and winter salivating while he wondered what it would be like to kiss her. Better yet, take her to bed and get nothing accomplished on the house at all. He'd have to be very, very careful.

"You're a fool, Cane," he told himself as he stood there. The night was warm and humid. Sweat poured off his face and chest. It rolled in a most uncomfortable manner down his back to his briefs. But the evening breeze that was picking up might have belonged to a cool October Halloween night from the shiver that went down his back. Not a light had been left on in the house, and the night-blackened trunks of the three front pines half hid the place, making it appear downright foreboding. Michael shivered again, wishing desperately he could call back their bid.

"This is nuts," he whispered out loud, there in front of the house. "I want this house, God only knows why. Candy's right. It reeks of family and commitment. With my family's track record, that's out for me. As far back as I know, none of them have managed to make a marriage last. God knows some of them tried often enough, too. I refuse to inflict what's got to be some kind of genetic flaw on some poor unsuspecting female. But look what I'm buying—and with whom! The original tempting morsel. Candy was probably an apple in the Garden of Eden in a former life. I just know it." She was beautiful. He'd gone so far as to ask her out, but that was before he realized what a prickly, competitive personality she had. There was certainly no way even a short-term alliance with her stood a chance.

42 HOUSEMATES

Michael moved around the house to the side entrance. This new perspective was no better. He tried to control a shudder, but couldn't quite manage. What a pit. So much to do. Lots of opportunities to get on each other's nerves. They'd have to set up some rules so they stood a chance of getting along if this thing came through. For one, there'd be no verbal free-for-alls of the type his parents had engaged in. He'd get a book. He was good at research. In fact, he'd seen a book just the other day: *Fight Right: The Layman's Guide to Getting A Point Across While Saving the Relationship,* or some such thing. Maybe he'd pick it up on his lunch hour tomorrow.

He sighed as he stared at the place. Well, it would work because he'd make it work. Every dime he'd saved from the moment he'd gotten out of school rode on it working.

He walked away from the house, his pace gradually picking up speed until, with a last pathetic glance over his shoulder, he broke into a jog and renewed sweating simultaneously.

"Working side by side with her fixing up that place is asking for trouble. She's got the body of a siren and the personality of a prickly pear. I'll be spending the next several months pulling little barbs out of my hide. But I'm aware of it, so I'll be on my guard. Besides, we may not get the house at all. Somebody else bid more. The whole thing will probably fall through." Michael felt much better by the time he reached his apartment. Tomorrow his biggest problem would be convincing Lorenzo's to help him make Golden Circle, he just knew it.

Life seldom went according to plan, and Michael knew he was in trouble when Candy bounced into the office around ten the following morning.

"Guess what, guess what, guess what!"

HOUSEMATES 43

Shoot. She was so excited, her *guess what*'s were exclamatory rather than interrogative. It could only mean... With a certain sense of inevitability, he asked, "We got the house, didn't we?"

"Yes, yes, yes!"

He'd cancel his call on Lorenzo's. Somehow he knew it wouldn't be productive. Not today. "You've been in the business world too long. You're starting to speak in triplicate." The muscles at the back of his neck were suddenly tense and his hand clenched into a fist all by itself. "You're positive?" he asked, hoping for some little hint of *maybe* hidden amongst all those yeses.

"I'm positive." She beamed, amazing him with the sheer number of blindingly white teeth she could show at once. "Mary called a little while ago and said so."

Michael's own teeth were clenched so tightly from nerves he was going to have to take a crowbar with him to pry them open when he went to the sandwich shop where he usually ate lunch. He was a doomed man. Doomed. "What, exactly, did Mary say?"

Michael had to trail after Candy as she did some kind of two-step jig across the room. She dropped her purse onto her desk chair and turned to face him. Putting both arms around him, she squeezed, hard.

Michael was left breathless, and it wasn't from her hug. Candy didn't have that much upper-body strength. At the moment he knew only one thing for sure. He was in deep trouble. Candy's body fitted against his as though engineered to exact specifications. At a guess, he'd say the error tolerance was less than for one of the robotics he designed for a living, and those were minute indeed. The pull he'd felt when he'd first met Candy had been as instantaneous and intense as it had been inexplicable. The light contact she'd just initiated let him know that it would be useless to try and convince himself the attraction was lessening with time and exposure. He simply wasn't ready for this. He took a deep breath and exhaled slowly. "What did Mary say? Her exact words."

"She caught me as I was on my way out the door to Riggins. Another couple of seconds and she would have missed me."

"Candy—" Michael began warningly.

"She said the listing realtor had just called and while one of the other bids was higher, they were giving it to us!"

Michael collapsed into the chair next to Candy's desk. "Another bid was higher, but we got the house? How is that possible?"

"Contingencies," Candy responded succinctly.

"Contingencies! What contingencies? We didn't have any. Our bid was so clean, it squeaked."

"I know, it was just like you said." Candy smiled approvingly down at him as she came to a breathless stop by her desk. "The heirs just want to take the money and run. The other offer wasn't that much higher and they stipulated that the whole house had to be cleaned out before they took possession. There's sixty-five years' worth of junk in that house."

He knew, he knew. Now *he* got to clear out sixty-five years' worth of crud. "Imagine the nerve."

"Yeah, well, it cost them the house. It's ours now. How's that for something meant to be?"

A certain fatalism took over. Maybe everything would work out. Maybe they'd make a million dollars on the thing and he wouldn't have to worry about work, promotions or commission checks ever again. Maybe the Cubs would take the World Series this year, too.

HOUSEMATES 45

"Michael, you look a little shell-shocked. Are you okay? Don't you see? We did it, Michael, you and me. We beat them all. We won."

Had they? He wondered.

"You are happy, aren't you?"

"Oh, yes. Happy. Very."

He could feel her eyes studying him.

"I don't understand— Oh, sure, yes, I do. Don't worry," she said soothingly. "It's probably buyer's regret. A classic reaction, really. It'll pass." She patted his arm. She actually patted him.

Candy was definitely mother material, he decided. She had that maternal tone used on fearful toddlers down pat. He refrained from pointing out that he was not a two-year-old. Things said in the heat of the moment were often regretted, after all. "Well." He sighed. "I guess we better order up that home inspection I wanted. I'll feel better once we know what the damages really are."

Of course, there was a fifty percent chance he'd feel a lot worse, too.

Candy checked her watch. "Good idea, but first we need to get over to the bank. We have to up the ante and raise our down payment to ten percent. I've got to move some money. How about you?" She looked at him expectantly.

Transfer funds. Right. He sighed. He pulled himself up and out of the chair. It was a difficult feat due to the lead ball lodged in the pit of his stomach. He was unsure of the origin of the pressing weight. Probably the knowledge that this funds transfer was the first finger prick to what would in all likelihood become a major hemorrhage in his savings account. The drive to the bank was accomplished in relative silence. As the teller efficiently handled the paperwork, Michael decided that he did not feel like an ebullient new entrepreneur in business at last. There was something about knowing that other people had wanted the house that had persuaded Candy it was perfect. Michael wished his doubts would vanish as easily. Maybe Candy was right. Maybe it was run-of-the-mill buyer's remorse and would pass. It felt more like severe depression.

Candy must have recognized the route he took away from the bank, but she said nothing until he slid the car next to the curb on the opposite side of the street from their new home, and Candy slid up against his back and pointed around him out the window. "Michael, look at it. Really look. Remember all the potential for charm you and Mary kept sticking my nose in? It's there. I can see it now. It's wonderful."

Michael didn't say anything. It had only been wonderful when it had remained an intellectual exercise. The reality of trying to pull this thing off was definitely not wonderful. He continued to stare out the side window. He wished he could think of something bracing to say. He didn't like Candy seeing him as anything but assertive and in control.

Candy persevered. "Picture those overgrown pines trimmed way up high, like you said, so that the house is visible from the street."

Michael tried. He screwed up his face and squinted through his glasses at the structure.

Candy put her hands on his shoulders, drawing him back in a gesture he guessed was meant to comfort. Could she really be so naive? He felt decidedly uncomfortable— even more so with every second she remained plastered against his back.

"I've given this a lot of thought," she told him. "Imagine the trim a rich gingerbread brown to complement the tan brick. We'll take down one or two of those side maples completely so the sun can dapple the windows. When they're clean, they'll sparkle with bits of sunlight.''

Michael squinted harder, trying desperately to visualize her verbal sketch, but the way she stayed snuggled up to his back had other, much more disturbing mental images interfering with those of a freshly painted house. He wished to God she'd say something annoying.

"We'll get the chimney cleaned. Since we'll be working through the fall and winter, it'll be nice to stop whatever we're doing now and then and light a fire in the living-room fireplace. We'll sit in front of it with a little wine and cheese or something."

Her voice crawled over and in him. She was kneading his back in an effort to loosen the knots of tension she must have found. He could feel his very bones begin to soften as she worked on them.

Yes. They'd sit in front of a fire. He'd get some kind of rug. He could picture it now. Fur, preferably white. He'd nibble cheese from her fingers and go right on down her arm to the more interesting parts of her body.

No, no, no! This was exactly what he had to avoid. This was a business deal, nothing more. He'd best remember that if he was to survive the next few months with his heart intact.

He cleared his throat and remained staring out the window, trying hard to concentrate. But her quintessentially female perfume invaded his nostrils, and his body was tensing all by itself.

Harrumphing, he could still detect a touch of desperation in his voice when he spoke. "Looks like they're going to leave those nice stone planters by the front patio there."

Candy grasped his shoulders to steady herself while she peered over him for a better view. "Where?"

He took a breath to calm himself. She didn't know what she was doing, he was almost sure of it. He pointed. "There. See? In between each set of French doors and on either side of the outermost ones."

"Oh, yeah. I see them." She was silent for a moment. "We'll fill them with plants in the spring. Something that likes shade. Impatiens or begonia."

Candy was close enough to be literally breathing down his back. He was so aware of her he fully expected a brand the size and shape of her body to remain on his back once she finally pulled away.

She had to know what she was doing. Didn't she? Maybe she wasn't thinking about what she was doing because she just didn't see him in that way. He supposed it was possible, although he'd been aware of her in that way since he'd first laid eyes on her. But he wouldn't react to it. He absolutely wouldn't.

Oh, Lord, he was dying. Heck, he'd died and was paying for every misdemeanor he'd ever committed. And the kicker was the instrument of torture hadn't a clue! It was all too much. "Surely we won't still be here come spring," he got out, extremely grateful his voice didn't squeak.

"Spring's the best time to put a house on the market," Candy countered. "We'll make the most money doing it that way. But I bet we'll both be surprised by the amount of time this all takes, especially as we plan on doing most of it ourselves. For all I know, it might take two or three times as long as we think."

It had better not. Not if he was to survive without losing his mind. He shivered. Damn. It was eighty-five degrees outside and he had the chills. "The . . . the grass has a lot of weeds. We'll have to do something about that." He was proud of himself for sounding even slightly coherent.

"So we'll get a bag of weed and feed."

HOUSEMATES 49

"One?" he questioned. More like ten. Man, this house better pay off big time. There'd better be some kind of major recompense for all the hard work he'd pour into it. And money, he reminded himself. Don't forget the money. His eyes swept the lawn one more time. There were a hell of a lot of weeds there for one piddling bag of weed and feed. How many of their other estimates had been more optimistic than knowledgeable?

"I know we don't close on the house for more than six weeks," Candy was saying when Michael focused back in on their conversation. "But I think it would be a good idea to talk things through. Lay down some ground rules, set priorities, that kind of thing."

"You've been in the business world too long. Should we do a flow chart of our plans while we're at it?"

Candy hit him and, thankfully, disengaged her front from his back. "Don't be facetious."

Taking a deep breath of relief, he questioned cautiously, "What kind of ground rules do you have in mind?"

"Oh, you know. The usual stuff."

"No, I don't know. Like what?" Michael started the car and after checking over his shoulder, pulled out onto the brick-paved street.

"Where are we going?" Candy asked.

"To the mall," Michael responded as he pulled off the side street and onto a main thoroughfare. "I thought we could check a couple of bookstores for some how-to manuals."

"Oh. Good idea. I haven't got anything on my calendar at work that can't be delayed."

"Good. Now about these ground rules . . ." He was almost afraid to hear. God only knew what her convoluted mind might cook up.

She shifted in the seat next to him. He was as aware of the small movement as if she'd unexpectedly jumped into his lap.

"It's just that several of my friends have already been through this kind of process."

"And?"

She twisted again. He wished to God she'd stop moving around and distracting him before he had an accident.

"Well, they all said that remodeling a house was a good way to end up in the divorce courts."

"But we're not married," Michael pointed out with unflattering haste. "So how can we get divorced?" He should be grateful Candy wanted to get along during what was sure to be a long-drawn-out process. Hadn't he gone and bought a book on that very subject? Instead, all he felt was panic. If she stayed prickly, he might stand a chance of hanging on to his heart, but if she suddenly went all agreeable on him ...

"I think what they meant was this kind of thing can get stressful. Unless both people make a real effort to not jump down each other's throats over every little thing, it can get very unpleasant, that's all."

Oh, that was all. "You're saying if I tiptoe around your delicate little ego so as not to bruise it, you'll tiptoe around mine?" He was needling her and he didn't know why. Probably a belated sense of self-preservation kicking in. Getting along with Candy could be a dangerous thing to do.

"No, no," she denied, obviously impatient with him already. So much for not jumping down each other's throats. "I'm saying if we both show some tolerance of each other, work hard and are willing to put in our fair share, in the end, we'll have something worth having. Something to be proud of."

HOUSEMATES 51

Thoughtfully Michael pulled into the first empty spot he saw in the mall parking lot. He looked at Candy. What she'd just described was exactly what he'd once intellectualized a good marriage should be. He hoped like hell Candy wasn't thinking along those lines. What with his parents being divorced—his mother twice—both sets of grandparents victims of marital malaise and three of his four great-grandparents having been separated or divorced, Michael figured he was a walking statistical time bomb. Odds for a successful marriage of a fourth-generation product of divorce were slim to nonexistent. He'd never been to Vegas. Never wanted to. He'd only lose. He could lose big time here, too, but only if he let himself.

But Candy looked so innocent sitting there. He must be overreacting. They'd been talking about the house, not the state of possible wedded bliss, after all. Surely Candy had no secret agenda. He'd know.

"I will make every effort to be tolerant and do my fair share," he pledged as he walked around the car to open her door. "I expect you're right. If we both work very hard at this, in the end we'll have something worth having." Provided they didn't waste a lot of time spinning their wheels and doing things half-assed backward. They definitely needed those self-help manuals. "Let's go on in."

"Psychology, travel, young adult. Um, self-help. There it is!"

Michael shook his head doubtfully. "No, I don't think so. This seems to be all personal stuff. How to do your own taxes, start your own business. Here's one on dressing for success, pleasing your sexual partner— Uh..." Michael cleared his throat and stepped uneasily toward the adjoining book rack. "There must be another—"

52 HOUSEMATES

"Over there. Look." Candy pointed as she took off down the main aisle of the bookstore. "Home and Home Improvements."

Silence prevailed in that section of the store for a full twenty minutes as they flipped through the pages of several books plucked from the shelf. Finally they spoke simultaneously for a few moments until Michael gave Candy the floor to speak.

"Listen to this and tell me if you understand a word of it. 'Two basic furnace duct systems are most frequently used. These are the radial and extended-plenum systems.' I thought radial referred to tires, and I've never even heard the phrase 'extended-plenum' before."

"I wonder if the wiring in that place is grounded."

"Listen to this—"

"No, you listen. I'm seriously concerned about the electrical wiring."

Candy shrugged off his concerns. "Wiring, shmiring. How bad can it be? It's lasted almost ninety years so far. I'm a lot more worried about the heating system."

"Hey, the heat goes out, you get a little cold. Bad wiring can short out and burn the whole place down," Michael responded without really looking up from his text. "How many amps—"

Candy snapped her book shut and replaced it on the shelf by forcing it between two other missives of a similar type. "Let's leave," she said. "I'm already getting a headache. There's got to be a simpler approach to handling this kind of project."

It was difficult to squeeze his own text back into the overloaded shelf, but Michael finally managed the feat. "Nothing has been simple since the moment I first laid eyes on that place," he complained.

HOUSEMATES

"All right, Michael, I'm officially declaring your time for buyer's remorse to be at an end. I have no intention of putting up with your sulking for the entire six months coming up."

"Oh, forget it," Michael said, disgusted with himself for overreacting. "You're right about one thing. These books aren't going to do us a damn bit of good unless we can find one that comes with an interpreter. I've never even heard of half of the *tools* they're talking about, let alone what we're supposed to *do* with them."

He took her arm and began guiding her out the store door, determined to leave the place before he made a bigger fool of himself. "Maybe we should go poke around a hardware store. At least then we'd have an idea of what some of this stuff looks like. Then we can decide if it looks like something we want to let into our lives."

"Isn't that sort of like closing the barn door after the horse is out?" Candy inquired as she let him lead her away. "I mean, the house is already ours. We're going to need those tools, whether we want them or not."

Life was like that, Michael mused as they wandered down the mall. Make one little move on the master chessboard and you were locked into ten or twenty moves you hadn't even considered when making the first one. All he'd wanted was a house. Just a nice little place to call his own. And what did he end up with? Half a house that he was fixing up for somebody else and, for all practical purposes, a wife for the next six or more months—the one thing he didn't want at all, ever. The logic of life absolutely defeated him at times.

"Come on," he growled. "Let's get a burger someplace."

Chapter Four

"He keeps talking about the importance of compromising," Candy complained to Tina several days later. "But the man doesn't know the meaning of the word."

Tina punched in a few numbers on her keyboard and waited to see what her computer made of them. "Sounds like you've got your hands full, all right," she agreed absently as she stared at her screen.

Candy sat back grumpily in her chair and folded her arms across her chest. "You can say that again."

"Sounds like—"

"That's not funny. He's got me half-crazed. One more pep talk on how we have to prioritize the tasks before us and work toward common goals and I swear, murdering him will be right at the top of my list of priorities."

"Look at it this way," Tina said sympathetically as she scrolled down a page on her monitor and typed in another set of numbers. "At least you're not married to him."

HOUSEMATES 55

"Might as well be," Candy grumped. "For all the effort I'm going to have to put into getting along with him the next few months, I might as well be. By the time this is over, my tongue'll be nothing but a stub from biting off everything rotten I'd like to say."

Candy was silent for a moment as she scanned her own monitor screen and found nothing to her liking. She picked up a pencil and pointed it at Tina. "And I'll tell you the worst part of it all . . ."

"What's that?" Tina asked as she bent forward and intently studied a line on her own screen.

Candy leaned across the space between their desks and whispered, "We'll end up working twice as hard as any married couple I know just to remain civil to each other, only we won't even get any of the side benefits, if you know what I mean."

And that nettled her. She didn't want to be aware of him in that way. But no matter how crazy he made her with his insistence the wiring came first, then the roof and boiler—when she knew darn good and well modernizing the bathroom and kitchen should take priority—she was unable to argue back effectively. For the first time in her life, a male's mere closeness had her so distracted it was impossible to effectively wage combat. Every time she took a deep breath to make a logical presentation of her viewpoint, the scent of his maleness filled her head and she found herself barely able to think at all. It depressed her, but she was coming to an understanding of couples who settled their differences in bed.

"But you didn't want any of those side benefits with Michael," Tina reminded her.

Candy had never realized how truly annoying her friend could be. "I know that. I still don't." Ha! "It's just that when you put this much effort into a relationship, you ought to get something out of it, you know?"

"Yeah, I know."

And Tina gave her a knowing look that made Candy want to smack her. She was appalled at the feeling. It was Michael's fault, of course. He was the one who had her emotions so out of control.

Tina continued, "But keep telling yourself you *are* going to get something out of this. You're going to walk away with the down payment in your hot little hands on the little bungalow you've been dying for. Stay keyed in to that and you'll be fine."

"You're right, of course," Candy said. "I've just got to hang on to that. Everything I've been working for so long is almost in my grasp. I can put up with anything a few more months."

And Candy tried to hold that thought as she and Michael spent the six weeks before the official closing wandering through stores. She took to keeping a small spiral notebook in her burgeoning purse, similar to one she'd noticed in Michael's briefcase. They both took them out and made notations whenever they roamed the aisles of a hardware store or a home-remodeling center.

Candy decorated the margins with arrow-pierced hearts and was always freshly irritated when she found herself starting another. They made lists. Copious lists. For that entire six-week period, their arguments centered on prioritizing the items on those lists.

She had to disguise her hearts by doodling heavily over them before she let him see her notes.

"What the heck is that?"

"What?" Candy asked innocently.

"That black blob taking over your paper."

"Nothing. Just . . . subconscious doodling. You know."

HOUSEMATES

"I think your subconscious is into violence. Look how heavy and dark that is. Your inner mind knows how silly this list is and has drawn a Sherman tank to shoot some of these entries down."

"And just what, might I ask, is wrong with this list?" Candy asked indignantly. A Sherman tank indeed. But she'd die before admitting it had started as a heart with an arrow.

"Oh, come on, Candy. Look what you've got on this thing. With all the major tasks we've got in front of us, I can't believe you're even giving kitchen curtains or towels space on the page." Michael all but snorted as he watched her mark them down one evening as they were passing through a department store's linen section.

Candy arched her brow in a superior fashion. It was tough to look down on somebody a couple of inches taller than she was, but hopefully he'd pick up on the impression of disdain, anyway. "Wasn't it you and Mary harping about how the listing realtor lacked vision? Both of you said most people did," she reminded him. "It only follows that adding the little extras that make a house appear homey and allow people to picture themselves in it will make them want to buy it. For example, a nice set of towels hanging in the bathroom is important, even though nobody's actually going to be living there while we're showing it."

"After we replace the wiring and heating systems, we'll gut the kitchen. But that's a ways down the road. There'll be any number of sales between now and the time we'll be ready for curtains in there. And could we worry about getting the bathroom into a usable state before we jazz it up with towels no one is ever going to use? You're the one who said a new ceiling in there would be nice. And you're right—the current one is falling down, as I recall. The ceramic tile is badly cracked and the toilet still flushes with an overhead pull chain.''

Candy eyed the linen display in front of them. ''Certainly curtains and towels are not of the same immediate priority as the bathroom ceiling, the boiler—or the wiring. This is a separate list I'm making.''

''What kind of separate list?'' Michael asked suspiciously.

''These are things we'll eventually need and should be keeping our eyes open for a good deal on them.'' She waved a hand toward a high mound of lace-edged terry cloth. ''Right now I'm thinking maybe we should pick up a set of these towels and put them away. They're on sale and this champagne color would go with almost any color wallpaper we decide to put in there.''

Michael immediately panicked. ''Wallpaper! I figured we'd just repair the walls and paint the whole place a nice off-white. You know, clean, bright, inoffensive and, best of all, cheap.''

Candy tested the towels' plushness with her hand. They were thick, soft and reduced for clearance. ''I think that would be a mistake,'' she argued back. ''Too sterile.''

Uneasily Michael watched Candy's hand caress the bath linens. His body was responding to the visual stimuli, much to his chagrin. He fought to concentrate on her warped thinking, instead. ''Sterile? What are you talking about now?''

''You heard me. Clean and inoffensive is all well and good, but what we're looking for here has to transcend that. We're looking for warmth. We want the buyer to connect with this house. The decorating we choose has to speak to them.''

He blinked at that. ''I beg your pardon?''

HOUSEMATES

Candy explained eagerly. "The way we decorate the place can allow us to subconsciously sway a potential buyer into feeling at home in our house and therefore be more eager to make a bid."

"It will?" He watched as she rooted through the stacks, pulling aside two of each size. A sense of edginess began nibbling at his nervous system. It was rapidly becoming a permanent condition around Candy. The woman could come up with more ways to spend money than any other three women he knew combined.

"Certainly." She had two bath and four hand. All she needed now was a couple of washcloths. "Hanging these towels in that bathroom, maybe putting out a little bowl of decorative soaps, will distract people from seeing how small the bathroom is. Instead, they'll focus on how cute it is and how much they want that bathroom for their own." She hugged the stack to her breast. Already she had no problem visualizing Michael stepping out of a steaming shower, wrapping himself in one of these plush babies and walking into the bedroom, a few beads of water still rolling slowly down his chest. Oh, God, she had no business thinking that way! Michael was off bounds. *Off bounds, do you hear?* she scolded herself.

Candy cleared her throat. "Uh, what I mean is—"

Michael had sensed a losing battle as Candy's personal stack grew. Why hadn't they discussed their priorities *before* they'd gone into this partnership? You know, sort of like an engagement before marriage—not that a lot of people took advantage of their engagements to really get to know the other person. Hormones, he concluded glumly, could trip a man up every time. "Never mind, I don't think I really want to understand."

"You're just being pigheaded. This is a family house. We have to make it appeal to them. Can't you just see some young mother sending a toddler in to wash up while she settles the baby in the nursery?''

Now she was talking about babies, for God's sake. His pulse raced a bit unevenly. He had to get a grip. This was all sounding too...good. "If we're sending toddlers in to wash up, we'll want navy blue towels, not beige. A kid would destroy these the first time he touched them."

A bit of firmness was called for here, he decided. "Candy, we're not buying those towels tonight. There will be other linen sales, if we decide at some much later date we can't live without them."

She rested her arm on the pile she'd created. "It seems to me, Michael, that you and I didn't spend enough time clarifying the basic approaches we wanted to take in this endeavor before we jumped into it." The more she thought about it, the more she realized that what was happening between them was similar to suddenly finding yourself married and realizing you never really knew the other person. Again, she could only thank God this was a temporary arrangement.

"Yeah, I know," Michael concurred gloomily. He was still having a bit of trouble ridding himself of a mental image of Candy as the young mother. Damned if the kid with the dirty hands didn't resemble himself a bit, too. He was not buying those towels. Not today, maybe not ever.

"Michael, I'm buying these towels. They're a good deal and worth putting away until we need them."

"No," he argued desperately. "I don't agree with your decision, and we have to be in consensus."

"Didn't I let you buy four different types of hammers in the hardware store last night?"

"Every one of those was a necessity," he protested indignantly. "We're going to need those hammers."

HOUSEMATES 61

"Nobody needs four kinds of hammers," she argued. "I'm buying these."

He was not a salesman for nothing. He would try negotiating a deal. "If you get to buy the towels, I get to go back and get the set of Phillips head screwdrivers I wanted."

"You already got the hammers. The towels are my tit for tat for letting you have those."

"Oh, no. Oh-h-h, no. You'll get to use the hammers, too. They're not just for me."

"Be still my heart." Candy crinkled her nose at him. "Just to show you what a sport I am—you being so generous with your hammers and, I presume, your Phillips screwdrivers set—I'll let you occasionally wipe your hands on one of my towels." With that she picked up her stack of towels and headed for the cash register.

He didn't want to *touch* those towels. He didn't even want to be in the same *room* with them. Michael followed quickly in her wake. This was not going the way he'd planned. She was supposed to see the error of her ways and bow to his greater wisdom. He didn't even want the stupid screwdrivers. Not yet, at any rate.

"Candy, wait. What if you find some clearance wallpaper somewhere? You know, the kind of stuff a store can't move—some weird shade of green with a white background."

Of course, he had no intention of okaying any wallpaper purchases, but he wasn't above dangling it in front of her to get his way. "It would be a shame not to be able to take advantage of a great deal like that. You'd have to tell yourself no because you'd be stuck with these towels. I mean, you couldn't use beige towels in a room with green-and-white wallpaper, now could you?"

62   HOUSEMATES

Candy never even paused. "Michael, I will have no problem walking away from a closeout on weird green-and-white wallpaper."

He put up his hands in a capitulating gesture. "Okay, okay. But I still say, if you buy those now you're committed to beige—"

"Champagne."

He looked doubtfully at the stack in her hands as she waited in the checkout line. "Champagne?"

She nodded. "Yes. Champagne."

His mouth quirked and his brow furrowed. She had to be kidding. "All right," he said slowly. "So you'd be committed to, uh, champagne. We might find some paint closeouts somewhere. You know, the custom-mixed mistakes? What'll you do then? We could save a lot by going with, oh, I don't know, gray trim. Then what?"

Candy handed her purchases to the clerk without even turning her head in his direction. He watched with a somewhat stoical expression as the towels were rung through, but he could not avoid wincing at least once. He decided there and then *he* would be in charge of receipts. If necessary, he'd sneak behind her back to return a few things.

Candy handed the woman her charge card and watched in satisfaction as the plastic was run through the machine. "I like the weird-green-wallpaper idea better than the gray-trim closeout," she finally said. "Gray has no warmth, you know?" Green was more vibrant. She could see Michael against green. Darn, there she went again.

Michael took several deep breaths. The woman was nuts. Unfortunately these six weeks they were spending in limbo had given him plenty of time to read his book on relationships. He'd given it to Candy, but right now it was looking doubtful she'd learned anything useful from it.

The author had stressed that to successfully build "intimacy," one could never, ever lose control. Things said in anger would never be forgotten or forgiven by the other person. He knew that was true from watching his parents. While this certainly wasn't as permanent as a marriage, he did want to get along for the duration of their agreement. So instead of telling her she was as crazy as a loon, he contented himself with, "I have to say I disagree with most of the basic premises you seem to be operating under today," and felt both put upon and noble.

The clerk handed the charge slip to Candy. She signed it with a flourish and handed it back. "When we're done here, we'll go back to the home-improvement center and buy one, I repeat, one Phillips head." Men were so pathetic when it came to hardware stores. Once inside, a woman was lucky to pry a man out in anything under an hour. Candy would never understand the male fascination with the monotonous rows of mysterious doohickeys or their willingness to part with large sums of cash to cart home bushels of oddball tools they'd never use, not even in several lifetimes.

"Have a nice evening," the clerk told them as she handed Michael the bag of linen.

Michael grimaced, but picked it up.

"You, too," Candy responded since Michael remained silent. Men! Who could understand them? Decorating centers and department stores were a lot more interesting than hardware stores. She sighed, knowing she'd have been much better off as far as her sanity was concerned if she'd shared this venture with another female. Dealing with Michael was going to compound the difficulty of making a go of this house thing. In fact, it was going to be darn hard work.

64   HOUSEMATES

Look at him. He wasn't even waiting for her to put away her charge card. He was already striding off. She sighed again, stuffed the bit of plastic away and hurried after him.

Michael brooded as he toted the bag of linens to the car. The bag's paper crinkled with every step he took, furthering his annoyance. When he was a few feet from his auto, he pulled the keys from his back pocket and jangled them until he'd located the trunk key. The trunk popped open about the same time Candy appeared beside him.

He glanced up. "There you are. What took you so long? See something else you wanted to get and put away?"

"Is that why you were walking so fast?" Candy asked. "Afraid of what I'd find on the way out if we left at a normal pace?"

Placing the towels inside, Michael slammed the trunk shut and turned to her, noticing her red face and labored breathing for the first time.

"You need to start exercising. Something aerobic for at least twenty to thirty minutes three days a week would take care of that breathlessness. Good grief, this wasn't more than a brisk walk, and the car wasn't parked all that far away."

Candy was insulted to the core. "I do exercise," she protested indignantly. "I am in terrific shape."

She had him there. Her shape was giving *him* more trouble than it was her. In fact, he'd have to insist she wear sacks, extremely baggy sacks, when they worked on the house together. "Then why are you huffing like that?"

Her breathlessness had little to do with physical conditioning and a lot to do with Michael. It was his sheer audacity that quickened her breathing, she assured herself. The breadth of his shoulders was absolutely not the reason. Neither was the way his well-worn jeans molded his legs and seat.

HOUSEMATES

For the umpteenth time she wondered why his business suits didn't show his body to the same advantage as his blue jeans. She could hardly wait to see him in nothing but those jeans and one of those cute carpenter belts with a hammer—or four—hanging from it. She could probably sell tickets. Shoot. Where were his glasses? Maybe if he put those on she wouldn't be so subject to whatever spell his brown eyes were weaving over her.

Grimly she shook her head to clear it. Then she felt her forehead. Maybe she was coming down with something. A good case of the flu would explain a lot. "Michael," she said slowly as she slid into the passenger seat of his car. "We need to talk."

Michael climbed in beside her. He inserted the ignition key, but didn't turn it. "Yeah? About what?"

"Us. The way we react to each other. Has it occurred to you that we seem to be basically incompatible?"

"No. I mean, no more than you'd expect a man and a woman to be."

"I'm serious. I'm not sure we're ever going to be able to see eye to eye on much of anything."

"But that's good." Or so he'd been trying to convince himself the past few weeks. "I mean, everything in life is a balancing act, you know what I mean? If we thought alike, we'd miss the flaws in each other's reasoning and probably make a lot of mistakes."

Candy groused, "The way we're going about it, we'll spend so much time trying to iron out our differences, we'll be paralyzed and never get anything done."

She wondered if Michael knew he'd let his arm drift across the back of the seat. It now rested behind her head and his hand was playing with her hair. In terms of erotic foreplay, it probably didn't rank terribly high, but it should. It was darned effective. She could recall very few times when she'd been so totally aware of a man.

"I've given this a lot of thought," Michael continued as he started the car and, using his free hand, drove away from the mall. "And you really don't want two people on a project with the exact same strengths and weaknesses. A couple should complement each other, not mirror one other."

"I don't think you have much to worry about," Candy muttered. "We're hardly mirror images of each other. I'm serious about this, Michael. Several of my married friends have done what we're attempting. Fixer-uppers were all they could afford. They said it was terribly stressful on their relationship. One couple actually went as far as contacting lawyers."

The thought of divorce sent a chill down Michael's back and renewed his determination never to get caught in the marriage trap in the first place. Still, he smiled gamely. "Seeing as how we're not planning on marriage, we won't have to worry about a divorce." He held up his hand. "But I understand what you're trying to say. I'm the one who gave you the book to read on getting along, remember? I know we don't want to turn these few months together into a living hell. We're both reasonably intelligent adults. I'm positive that if we put our minds to it, we can get along for the limited time necessary to get this house done and sold. We'll each have what we wanted from the deal then." He hoped. "And we'll be able to go on our separate and merry ways with hopefully only a few scars, physical or mental, to show for it."

The ride back to their apartment building was done in silence, and Michael left her at her door. He was afraid to ask to come in for coffee. Afraid of where it would lead.

HOUSEMATES 67

* * *

Candy gave little thought during those weeks to the amount of unnecessary time they were spending together. She sat beside him on the front seat of his car over and over again while he zipped in or out of some parking lot. She felt an odd contentment as they bantered their way up one aisle of a hardware store and down the next. The thrill of victory when she convinced Michael to limit his screwdriver purchases to two Phillips heads and three regular in a variety of sizes buoyed her mood. That lasted all the way until they ran into an arts-and-crafts fair at the mall one weekend where Michael, rather autocratically in her opinion, refused even to consider a purchase of a beautiful painting that would have been perfect hanging above the living-room fireplace—eventually. Reluctantly she walked away. She'd gotten her way with the towels, after all.

Candy thought of this period as a time of necessary preparation. Her notebook was virtually filled with illegible scrawls that made no sense when she went back and tried to decipher them. Of course, she might have been more successful at the task without Michael hanging over her shoulder still trying to psychoanalyze her doodling.

"Wow, good thing you didn't major in fine arts. Look at this one. What the heck is it—a steamroller? Some kind of heavy earth-moving equipment, for sure."

Candy glanced between him and her heavily scratched-out heart floating with little or no grace on the margin of her paper. "I told you," she hissed. "I don't know what it is. It's subconscious. My hand just does it."

"You're so petite and delicate. It's hard for me to associate you with a subconscious that comes up with such heavy dark blobs. I guess I would have expected something much lighter and airier. Line drawings of bows with

68 HOUSEMATES

little birds pulling on the streamer ends, or maybe flowers encased in hearts."

Michael thought she was delicate. Petite. She'd been handed plenty of more flowery compliments by members of the opposite sex, mostly after a date, when they were angling for more than a good-night kiss. Michael's compliment had her straightening her spine and pushing her shoulders back, ridiculously pleased. She'd calmly closed the door in the faces of those other men. She hoped Michael never tried to push her, because she doubted she'd get off so easily with him.

"Thank you." She smiled, letting the stupid part about the birds and bows go by. After all, he'd been right about the hearts.

Michael's buyer's remorse still lived, but it now resided in a back corner of his mind with an only occasional foray down into the pit of his stomach. He was no longer convinced he was going to lose his proverbial shirt on the project. People made money all the time with deals like this. If the two of them lived through the ordeal they, too, would make a killing. He was enjoying their outings. That fact made him nervous, but not enough to stop. Candy was only occasionally difficult—imagine, two hundred and fifty dollars for a piece of artwork neither could use once the house was sold—and he'd handled that. Life was good.

But no matter how you counted it, the six-week "honeymoon" only lasted forty-two days. It seemed there'd barely been enough time for the charge bill for the screwdrivers to come before Michael's car was parked in front of not another hardware store or home-decorating center, but *the* house. It was theirs, complete with gilded walls and radiators, scorched pots still on the stove and vandal-smashed mirror shards glittering on the floor. And, oh,

HOUSEMATES 69

Michael reminded himself, let us not forget any attendant ghosts the neighborhood children had conjured up.

They walked up the sidewalk. Michael wondered if Candy realized she'd taken his hand. The strength of her grip surprised him. She'd been so upbeat since the acceptance of their bid he hadn't expected nervousness.

The trek up the front sidewalk took forever. It felt almost ritualistic, like a walk down a church aisle. Candy's keeping step by his side as he went toward this new set of responsibilities didn't help the image in his mind, but it did feel right. *This is only temporary,* he reminded himself. *Don't go getting yourself all worked up over nothing. It all ends in a few months. Nothing here is permanent.*

Besides, there was no getting out of this. The deed was done. There was no going back. Their path was chosen. He ran out of trite adages about the same time they ran out of sidewalk.

In one of those moments that seems to stand apart from time, they stood at the front door, gazing up at the edifice before them. He was acutely aware when Candy wet her lips with her tongue as she cleared her throat.

Chapter Five

"Michael?" she finally said.

"Yes?"

"This is it. The moment we've been waiting and planning for."

Funny. He'd had no idea she had a flair for the dramatic. Of course, until now, he'd had no idea he did, either. One of those moments of self-discovery, he guessed. "Yep. Sure is."

They paused there in front of the door, Michael hesitant to spoil the drama of the moment by actually opening the door with the key the selling realtor had provided a short while ago at the closing.

Instead, he glanced around. Yes, he thought, God was certainly in His heaven. And evidently in high humor, to boot. The sun absolutely beamed down on the house's— now his—thin grass, on his sickly, spiky pine trees and on his peeling paint trim. Lordy, lordy, it was going to take

HOUSEMATES

quite an effort to resurrect this abomination, but it was his—ah, theirs, all theirs.

Michael used the key, then his shoulder, to open the front door. Resisting the urge to pick Candy up and carry her, instead, he put a hand at the small of her back and gently propelled her over the threshold. "Come on. Let's see how well our memories have served."

The entry hall was gloomy and dark. He felt Candy shiver and put an arm around her. There were goose bumps on her arm. It would be folly to assume she was responding to his closeness, but it would be reassuring to know he wouldn't be the only one struggling through the next few months.

"My goodness," she said, rubbing her arms and stepping away from him. "Brick must insulate really well. It's cool in here."

Really? He'd felt a heat flash when he'd touched her. He decided to concentrate on the gloom, rather than the temperature, and flicked the light switch next to the door.

Nothing.

Stepping away from Candy in order to cool off a bit, he covered his eyes for a moment with his hand, forcing the pupils to quickly dilate, then searched the ceiling. "Damn. Looks like vandals smashed the light fixture."

Candy sighed. "We didn't think to bring any light bulbs, did we?"

Her voice shook a bit. Probably she was still cold. Michael, on the other hand, felt warm enough to heat the place by himself. Strictly as a noble and selfless gesture, he tucked her back into his side. She voiced no complaint to the arm across her shoulders as he directed the way into the living room. The three double sets of arched French doors provided natural lighting in there.

72   HOUSEMATES

"Man alive," Candy murmured. "Could they have done a better job of trashing the place?"

Michael grimly surveyed the knee-deep garbage in the cavernous room. "They were certainly thorough," he agreed. "I don't remember it being this bad." He'd been too busy fighting his attraction to Candy and disagreeing with her initial assessment of the place, admittedly just to be difficult, to notice much else. "I wonder if the vandals came back since the last time we were here."

"We need to call for a Dumpster."

"We need to get a phone to do that."

"You need a phone to call for a phone."

Michael took a calming breath. "All right, no problem. I'll call from my apartment."

"It's Saturday. There won't be anybody to take your order."

Candy, it seemed, was not above being difficult just to be difficult, either. He would try nose-breathing to stay calm. "Okay, I'll call from the office on Monday."

"You've got meetings scheduled all day Monday."

"Then you can make the call."

"I've got meetings—"

He lost it. "Dammit anyway. Do you have to be so annoying?"

She placed her fingertips against her chest in a gesture of innocence. "Annoying! I'm not being annoying. I was merely pointing out—"

"All right, all right," Michael interrupted, exasperated with both himself and Candy. They couldn't afford such verbal sparring this early in the relationship. "Let me rephrase what I said. Uh…Candy, when you respond to my every comment with some negative reason why my idea won't work without presenting a viable alternative, I feel

HOUSEMATES

irritated.'' He held his palm up in her direction, indicating he was turning the floor over to her.

Candy stared at him blankly, taken aback. "I beg your pardon?''

He looked at her expectantly. "Don't you get it?''

"Get what? That you've suddenly gone totally weird?''

His irritation was back in a flash. "No. I've rephrased what I had to say into a calm, specific rejoinder that stays focused on what was bugging me, rather than letting our, uh, discussion degenerate into a name-calling confrontation taking place on a personal level.''

He looked so pleased with himself, as though he expected applause. Candy almost didn't have the heart to let him know she was clueless as to his point. "What's the difference?'' she finally said. "You're still telling me off.''

Michael wondered why he bothered. "Listen, maybe you prefer verbal free-for-alls, I don't know. I grew up with them, and believe me, they're not all they're cracked up to be. They've left me with an absolute abhorrence for scenes. Anyway, you're the one so worried about your friends and their almost divorce. I was simply trying to employ the rules of fair arguing so that we could make it through the next few months and possibly still be speaking to each other at the end of all this.'' For some indecipherable reason, he *wanted* to still be speaking to her at the end of all this.

"Well, I think it's stupid. It seems like splitting hairs to me.''

Michael spoke through gritted teeth. His arm had long since been removed from Candy's shoulder. Let her freeze. "Candy, what I am hearing you say is that you think my honest attempt at getting along together is stupid. I feel put down.''

Candy rolled her eyes, "Oh, for— That's not what I—"

"It's what I heard," he challenged, facing her with his arms across his chest.

"Michael," Candy stated, mimicking his posture, "when you continually interrupt and don't allow me to finish a sentence, I feel exasperated."

He nodded his acknowledgment. "Fine. I will try not to do that anymore. Now, my book says that when an argument is over, it's over, and I declare this one at an end."

Candy felt as if she was in the living room with a stranger. Where had this new Michael come from? He was so serious, so intent on following some kind of oddball set of rules. She shook her head in amazement. "Michael, I can't believe you read a book on how to argue in preparation for a home-remodeling project," she said.

"Well, I did," he returned, kicking a curtain torn down by the vandals out of his way as he went farther into the room. "Now, do you have any concrete suggestion as to something we might be able to accomplish as long as we're here?" He was thinking in terms of the world's largest temper tantrum, but first they'd have to clear out the room so there was enough space to throw it. He wouldn't want his style cramped.

"We packed a broom and some trash bags," Candy recalled slowly. "The bags are pretty useless to deal with the size of this mess, but we could sweep everything down to one end in preparation for the Dumpster."

Doubtfully, Michael checked the scope of the disaster facing them. They should buy a wheelbarrow that afternoon. Once the large stuff had been carted into a pile, a broom might prove useful, but not now. "Maybe later."

He took Candy's arm and guided her up the five steps to the dining room, which stood balconied off the living room like some ancient exotic tiered garden waiting for an archaeologist to dig out and restore. The ceiling there bowed over their heads. Michael kicked a scorched pot back through the doorway and into the kitchen. "There," he grunted. "At least it's in the right room."

Candy listened to the clatter and sighed. "If we'd thought to bring dust masks, we could have used the broom handle to knock this ceiling down. I don't think we've planned very well, Michael."

That wasn't quite true. They just needed to find something that needed hammering or screwing. They'd have to uncover it first, though. He planted his hands on his hips as he slowly pivoted in a circle. "The spring market starts picking up in February. It's already October," he informed her morosely. "I wish to God this place had come on the market a little bit sooner or that we'd been able to take possession a bit earlier. The way it stands now, even if we work every night and weekend, finishing it in time to catch the prime market is iffy at best."

Candy spread her arms out, hands palm down in a calming gesture. "All right. The thing to do is stay cool. We can't let ourselves get all overwhelmed. We'll break things down into smaller doable tasks and not even think about the big picture."

"Get through today and worry about tomorrow tomorrow?" Michael asked with a grim grin.

"Exactly," she said as they moved into the kitchen. "Now, in my expert opinion, we need to make a list."

"Another one?"

"Yes," she confirmed. "I'll get my notebook. There's something we actually have with us. It's in my briefcase out in the trunk."

Michael kicked the pot again. Candy jumped when it clattered against the wall. "No," he stated defiantly. "No more lists. Action. Pick a room, any room, and we'll go for it."

Candy would have argued, but it was clear Michael was not in the mood to entertain counterproposals. She glanced around at the ancient homemade kitchen cabinetry and the leftover linoleum flooring that had been used on the countertops. Formica must have still been only an ant's worst nightmare back then. She bet those little critters were glad formic acid was artificially produced now. She shook her head impatiently. At any rate, the room needed gutting. Surely even Michael could see that. Putting it back together might require some planning and foresight—a list or two—but surely the tearing apart could be handled without further ado.

And Michael was right about one thing. They'd made enough lists to paper the kitchen. "All right. Let's get the worst over with and do the kitchen first."

Michael immediately contradicted her choice. "What about something easy to give ourselves a boost? I vote for the living room."

Candy arched her eyebrows imperiously. She should have known he wouldn't be content to accept her choice. Men were so difficult. Her father was the same way. He usually deferred to her mother for a decision, then it fell to her mother to make sure she came up with the right choice. Otherwise, it turned out he'd merely been asking for an opinion. "The bathroom," she tried, willing to defend her choice this time. "With the hours we'll be putting in here, we're going to need to use one occasionally, and it's positively primitive up there, as well as gross."

Fixing up the bathroom held little appeal for Michael, either. It was going to require a *lot* of hard work. A hefty proportion of the chipped and cracked wall tile had given up in discouragement and fallen in disgrace from the wall.

HOUSEMATES

What remained would have to be chiseled off. All the fixtures needed replacing. He'd never reseated a toilet in his life. No, he'd rather delay that little project as long as possible. Maybe picking a room hadn't been such a great idea. There had to be some kind of warm-up activity they could do. Something to get them into the mood without half killing them. "Now that I think about it, isn't there a limit on the amount of time you can keep a Dumpster? Once it's delivered, I guess we'd better clear out as much stuff as possible. It would be great if we could empty the entire first floor, wouldn't it?"

Now who was being difficult? Candy's head was cocked to the side and her hands were on her hips. Her foot tapped as she gave him a look of disparagement.

Michael knew immediately she was on to his tricks. He broke into rueful laughter. The humor was infectious. Candy found herself grinning and then chuckling herself. The rich timbre of his laugh caught her by surprise. Unexpectedly, it brought out in him that other level of maleness. Not the one that had women shaking their heads in exasperation down through time, but the one that attracted and held them, despite the difficulty of ever understanding such an alien creature as man.

Michael's laughter stopped as he became fascinated by the slight one-cheek-only dimple Candy displayed when she smiled. The crushing sense of hopelessness that had weighed him down since entering the house lifted, then disappeared entirely when Candy reached for his hand and squeezed. It was a gesture of reassurance, nothing more, but Michael felt much more. He squeezed back, then dropped his arm to her waist. It felt right.

"Hey," he said. "We'll be fine."

"You know?" she came back. "I rather think we will."

He gave her bottom a friendly pat as he dropped his arm and marveled at her firm roundness. Damn, she was cute. He hated that she was cute. They'd only been inside the house fifteen minutes and already he needed to get away before he did something stupid. "Come on," he said firmly. "We're going out for Chinese. Then we'll worry about ordering a Dumpster, getting a phone and picking up a wheelbarrow so we can start to move all this junk."

Candy leaned back against one of the cabinets and looked up teasingly. "Chinese, huh? I'm in the mood for Italian."

Michael growled low in his throat and gave in to a sudden urge to kiss her.

He'd meant it to be brief, friendly, but it quickly escalated as he found himself using his tongue to trace the outline of her lips. Then he tried to coax her into parting her lips.

She sighed as his tongue played around her mouth, and that was all the entrée he needed. He deepened the kiss and reveled in the way she clung weakly to him as his tongue stroked the interior of her silken mouth. Somehow, knowing she was as enslaved by the same inexplicable attraction he felt made him feel better, and he smiled reluctantly when he finally regained enough control to pull his lips off hers. "Chinese—"

"Sounds wonderful," Candy admitted, sounding a bit dazed.

The breathy quality in her voice pleased Michael. And he *was* in the mood for Chinese.

Candy went through the weekend in a fog. Michael hadn't tried to kiss her again, but Sunday night she was still feeling the effects of his earlier spontaneous display. It had singed her nerve endings and interfered with her brain function. That had to be the explanation for the way she'd let him push her around all weekend.

She stood in the living room of their house and attempted to straighten her spine, then groaned. "Michael, we've got to talk," she announced as she tried to twist an arm behind her back to massage a sore spot. It wasn't worth the effort. She slumped onto the bottom step that rose from the living room up to the dining room.

Michael finished locking the French doors. A loaded Dumpster sat out in the driveway behind them now. Luckily, they had managed to find a waste disposal company that would deliver a Dumpster on the weekend. With a satisfied expression, he turned to her. "About what?"

"Do you even realize what a paragon of virtue I've been all weekend? Cooperation has been my middle name. It's got to stop."

He arched a brow.

"Don't give me any of your looks, either. I mean it. I've come to the conclusion you are not mortal." She glared at him accusingly. "God, I need a cup of coffee right now, but you've taken even that simple pleasure away," she grumbled.

"Candy, what are you talking about?"

"I'm talking about the fact that you've half killed me this weekend. More than half. I can't get up off this step to go get the coffee."

"Ah." Michael nodded his head sagely. "You're a little stiff. Look at it this way. You won't have to pay to go to a health club for a while."

Candy groaned. " 'Stiff' does not begin to cover what I feel right now."

"But look at all the progress we made."

Taking great care to move slowly, Candy reached down with her hands and laboriously lifted one leg and crossed it over the other. "Drop dead, Michael." She carefully leaned back against the newel post and sighed.

"I want you to know that if I ever come face-to-face with whoever wrote that book on getting along you've been incessantly quoting all weekend, I'm going to punch his lights out. I don't want to hear another word about us being partners or going the extra mile, understood? It's making me paranoid, what with you watching your every comment and tiptoeing around like I was made of glass and would shatter if you accidentally offended me. You've worked so hard to make sure you did your part that I'm exhausted trying to keep up. Every time I stop for a drink of water, I feel guilty." Her arms flopped a bit, all the gesture she was capable of right then. "Another weekend of this, and I'm a dead woman."

Michael stood there, gazing down at her wilted figure, bewildered. "I will never understand women," he finally announced. "I was trying to make sure you didn't regret going into partnership with me—making sure you got your money's worth, so to speak." He threw up his hands. "Women! I'm too tired myself to go brew coffee, but stay there. I'm pretty sure there's a couple of cans of cola left." When he came back, he picked up Candy's limp hand and wrapped it around the cold can. "Okay, go on. Any other complaints?"

"Yes, as a matter of fact there are. Yesterday. Eight o'clock in the evening. We hadn't eaten since noon. I was starving by then. You told me to go by myself. Bring you back something if I thought of it. Naturally I had to say I really wasn't that hungry and keep working."

With effort Candy hefted the can. The small sip she managed braced her enough to recross her legs in the opposite direction. She groaned as she attempted a second meditative sip.

HOUSEMATES

81

"I didn't get anything to eat until after eleven," she informed him darkly.

"I can see that coming between you and food is a mistake."

"What do you fuel your body with?" Candy asked. "Air?" She was so tired she was becoming incoherent. "I mean, come on, your shoulders are almost as wide as you are tall, so I know you're putting something in there."

Michael's eyes widened and he almost choked mid-colaswig. Candy thought his shoulders were broad? Did that mean she liked them?

"I saw that," she complained. "You just pushed your shoulders back and straightened up. Don't deny it. You did it on purpose, I know. And don't try to slump now. It's too late. By the way, as long as we're on the subject," she continued aggressively, "there's to be no more kissing or...or leaning over coolers to get pop. From now on, I'll get the pop. You're just trying to make sure I notice your unbelievable rear. Well, I noticed, so you can stop."

"What's that supposed to mean? There's nothing wrong with my butt." He ran a lot of miles to keep his butt in shape. She better not have any complaints on that score. He checked over his shoulder and it looked all right to him, but then again, his mind didn't operate from a female perspective.

"I know. That's what bothers me about it. Why, every time you leaned over to shovel stuff into that wheelbarrow, my pulse— I could feel it in my temples . . . and then, your arms . . . They *bulged* when you pushed it out to the Dumpster. I couldn't stop *staring,* and—"

Michael broke into laughter. Exhaustion had made the woman punch-drunk. "Candy, listen to yourself."

82   HOUSEMATES

She flushed as she realized what she'd been saying. "Well, I . . . that is, you . . . do you lift weights or something?"

Michael leaned down and hoisted her to her feet. "Come on, I'm taking you home. You need sleep. I'm sorry if you felt put upon this weekend. I'll make sure we break and eat at mealtimes from now on. I'm glad you like my shoulders, happy that my rear is a source of inspiration to you, and I think, come morning, you're going to be very upset that you let your mouth run away with you." He, on the other hand, had found it both revealing and fascinating. It was heady stuff indeed to know that Candy liked what she saw when she looked at him. After all, his reflection in the mirror had never excited him, and he was well aware he only achieved six-foot status in his dreams. Candy's confession was unexpected but definitely not unappreciated, although it did complicate things between them.

"I just don't like it when I find myself looking after you," she complained as Michael steered her out of the room.

"I know," he soothed. "I don't like finding myself looking after you, either."

"Do you, Michael?" she asked wistfully. "Do you look after me?"

"Sometimes," he admitted. More than he ought to if they were to stay uninvolved. "Now, get in the car and close your eyes. I'll wake you when we're back at the apartment building."

"There are certain jobs," Michael pontificated as he and Candy carried buckets and scrub brushes into the house the following evening, "that just won't be possible to do ourselves. We're going to have to pay professionals, and the pain won't be lessened by waiting. We may as well call

HOUSEMATES 83

them all in right now and get it over with. Did you remember the soap?"

Their footsteps echoed eerily in the now empty living room. Candy shivered. Just being back in the room embarrassed her. Michael had been right about that. Tonight, for some reason, she felt like crying. *I can't do this,* she told herself. *It's not possible.* "I've got the box right here, Michael, tucked under my arm."

"Good." He grunted. "Probably use up the whole container just in the dining room."

Candy looked at him, poised halfway up the stairs to the dining room. The dim light shining from the wall sconces was enough to cast several eerie shadows on his form. The tarnished gold of the once snazzily gilded walls behind him gave him the appearance of an angel fallen from favor. She didn't want to like him, but darn it, she did. And she knew with sudden clarity that, whatever it took, they would get through this. He was counting on their success as heavily as she was. She couldn't let him down. If they both lost their sanity trying to deal with each other and this crumbling edifice simultaneously, so be it. The house would be redone.

She straightened her shoulders and followed him up the stairs. "Maybe we could check into buying in bulk. Which jobs do you want to call in contractors for?"

Her voice was soft, even a bit tremulous, and Michael gave her an odd look before answering.

"Here," he said. "Give me that stuff. I can manage all of it. You still stiff?"

"Some." She didn't want to get into a rehash of the night before. "Oh, good. The mop's right where I remember leaving it. That doesn't often happen with me. We can do the floors when we're done with the walls. Now, you were saying?"

"You have to be licensed for electrical work, and neither one of us are. Then we'll definitely need a new boiler. Might as well get it done now before the really cold weather," he said as he began running water into a bucket. He added a healthy amount of cleanser and watched the water start to foam.

"Are you sure we need a new boiler? I mean, the one down in the basement has held up this long, don't you think it could make it another few months? Let the new people worry about it."

"Believe me, Candy, the men, at least, will head for the basement and check out the boiler and the circuit-breaker box. All the homey decorating in the world won't count for diddly squat if the main stuff isn't in good shape and of good quality."

She didn't know if he was right or not, but she had done some investigating. "Michael, I've made some calls. You're talking around two thousand dollars for a new heating system. You can buy an awful lot of paint and wallpaper for that kind of money. I'm convinced if the place is decorated to the nines, some young couple will walk in here and get hooked. They'll be so in love with the house itself they'll be willing to take a chance on an older boiler. But," she said, not wanting only the second item on the list to escalate into another major argument, "I'll think about it. What else do we need a contractor for?"

She hefted the full bucket out of the sink and lugged it into the dining room and up a ladder. Dunking a scrub brush, she carefully started in the upper left-hand corner of one wall.

"The roof," he stated definitively, running water into a second bucket.

"The roof?"

"Yes. The roof. Have you got a problem with that?"

HOUSEMATES 85

Candy rubbed her forehead. A definite tension headache was taking root. "No, of course not. One look at the water-damaged ceilings upstairs, and you know it's bad. Roofs are expensive, though. I just kind of thought we'd do it ourselves," she offered tentatively.

"Us?" He sounded perplexed. Obviously, he'd never even entertained the idea. "Have you lost your mind?" He brought his bucket in, sloshing water on the floor as he came. He started scrubbing in the dead center of the wall next to hers.

Good grief. He was so upset he'd even forgotten all his silly rules for constructive arguing. "Remember," she took delight in saying, "things said in the heat of the moment can never be taken back. Wouldn't it be better to start in a corner? And you're dribbling all over the floor," she commented as she observed his technique.

Michael parked his gorgeous rear on the radiator in back of him, ignoring the discomfort. He crossed his arms and glared up at her. "So the floor is dirty, too. I'm getting a head start on it," he informed her.

"You're making a mess, is what you're doing." Candy climbed down from the ladder and carefully moved it two feet to the right.

Michael pushed away from the radiator, exhaled audibly and turned his back on her. His hands, hanging stiffly at his side, clenched and unclenched several times. "You wash walls your way, I'll wash them mine."

"Well, I— Michael?" She stopped, bucket in hand, to watch him.

"Shh. I'm counting."

"Counting?" she repeated blankly.

"The book says, when you're in danger of losing it, to stop, take a deep breath and count to ten before you respond."

86 HOUSEMATES

That intrigued her. "Really? I thought that was one of those old bits of folk advice with no basis in reality. Is it working?"

"I wouldn't know," he responded overpolitely, his back still to her. "I haven't managed to get past four. Now, do you mind?"

It was hard to believe a grown man would actually go to such lengths. She, too, inhaled deeply. "No, Michael, be my guest. You go right ahead and count."

"Thank you," he responded gravely.

She watched in silence as his fists clenched rhythmically several more times and was so mesmerized by the way his arms corded into tense muscle and sinew with each flex, she jumped in surprise when he pivoted back around, and a bit of her own water sloshed onto the floor.

"Now, about the roof," he stated matter-of-factly, as if he hadn't spent the past minute or so staring out a window framing nothing but a night-blackened view. "It's simply not possible for us to do it ourselves."

"Why not?" she questioned brightly, perching back on her ladder. "Think of the money we'll save." That ought to appeal to him. "We'll get one of those long extension ladders and you can go up there and shuck off the old shingles with a pitchfork. I watched the roofers at my parents' house a couple of years ago. It didn't look all that difficult."

"Oh, really." Broodingly, he dunked his brush back in the bucket, then scribed another huge dripping arc on the wall in front of him. "I'll tell you what," he countered. "I'll agree to doing it ourselves if you're willing to go up on the roof with the pitchfork. That would leave me down below where I could break your fall if you slip, and I could also put the shingles in the Dumpster."

Candy was amazed by Michael's skewed view of life's proper order. "That's ridiculous. You'll be up. I'll be down."

"Why?"

"Why? Because...because you're the man. That's why."

Michael shook his brush at her. Water sprayed everywhere. "You'd have a fit if anyone said something like that in the office. I'm not going up there."

She pointed at the floor. "You need to mop up some of that water before the floor warps." Her bottom lip curled out mutinously when Michael just looked at her. "And why can't you go up?"

A bit viciously in her opinion, he attacked the wall once more with the brush. The man had no finesse, for sure.

"I'm afraid of heights."

Eyes rounded incredulously, Candy protested, "No. I don't believe it. You're a m—"

"Don't say it," Michael warned. "Just accept that I will only go up on a steep two-and-a-half-story roof if you go up with me. There, I'm done with this wall."

Done? He'd barely touched it. All he'd done was drown the floor. "You missed the corners. All four of them," she informed him. Scowling, she decided to try some of his own technique on him. "What I'm hearing you say is that my input on this damn list will not be weighted as heavily as yours and that you are not interested in curbing expenses on this project."

The rat looked her in the eye and came right back with, "I feel you're misinterpreting my remarks. I am afraid of heights, always have been, ever since Billy Finklestein talked me into jumping off the roof of his garage when we were ten. Broke my shoulder and my arm in three places. You can't believe how hot summer can get until you spend it encased in plaster down to your waist." He shrugged. "I

88 HOUSEMATES

have no hidden agenda other than an unwillingness to repeat that experience. I am, however, detecting a note of sexism in your unwillingness to perform your half of a task simply because, traditionally, the role of roofer has not been performed by females. I'm hearing that you'll consider me less than manly if I don't jump right up and take care of this. And who cares if I missed a spot here and there? It's all going to get covered with paint, anyway."

Well. Had she been put in her place or what?

Candy thought wistfully of all the money they could save if they took care of the roof themselves. An awful lot of paint and wallpaper, curtain fabric and tools could be bought with it. Unfortunately Michael was not about to be pushed into falling in with her brilliant scheme.

Michael, she was rapidly discovering, was not particularly biddable.

She caved in. "Oh, all right." She took a deep breath and exhaled slowly. "Tomorrow morning I'll call a couple of roofing places for estimates."

Michael looked at her uncertainly for several moments, as though waiting for a catch somewhere in her capitulation. Evidently deciding not to look a gift horse in the mouth, he nodded his head and merely said, "Thank you, Candy. I appreciate your understanding." After another few seconds, he added, "I'll rewash this wall, if it'll make you happier."

She nodded. "It would. I guess I have a hang-up about corners and I did read someplace that paint sticks better to a clean surface. I should warn you, though, I'm still not convinced about the boiler."

He understood. "Fine. We'll work on converting each other over to our own points of view tomorrow. Maybe we should call Mary Frank back. She's a realtor. She'd know

HOUSEMATES

how much a buyer would weight the age of the boiler in their decision to buy.''

Candy blinked. "Oh. Good idea. I'll also check with my friends who've done this kind of thing. See what they did.''

Michael approved. "Good thinking.''

They scrubbed, if not companionably at least quietly, for a few minutes. Candy refrained from pointing out that his water needed changing. She changed hers and hoped he got the idea. It worked.

"Candy?''

"Hmm?''

"Did you eat something before you came over, or do you want to stop for a bit and grab something? We can take a break if you want.''

Candy turned away from her wall and looked at him. Darned if he wasn't trying to be thoughtful. She nodded once. "Thanks. Let's do that. I'm not terribly hungry, but I have some pop and pretzels out in the trunk of the car that I threw in just in case we wanted a snack.''

"Give me your keys and I'll get them. You can stay here.''

She stared after his retreating back. *They'd just had a major argument. Michael's dumb rules had gotten them through it. They'd reached a workable compromise and were still speaking to each other. Well, she'd be darned!*

Chapter Six

Candy blew into the office the following afternoon on a gust of late-October air. Several colorful leaves from the row of sugar maples shading the parking lot rustled in with her. She pushed the door shut against any more and scooped the successful intruders up in her hands.

She carried them to her desk and dropped them from a point high above her trash can. They drifted down as she watched. Their carmine color stood out boldly against the charcoal carpet below. Beautiful.

So why didn't she feel aesthetically soothed?

She sighed. Only two of the five landed in the can. The others settled onto the carpet by her feet, looking bold and daring but out of place in the refined environment of a professional office. Candy sat in her chair and leaned over far enough to gather up the uncooperative leaves. Holding them in her hand, she studied them.

Their graceful curving forms, so different from the linear office environment of intersecting horizontals and

HOUSEMATES

verticals, spoke to her of nature and the cycle of seasons. Somehow, from there, her thoughts jumped to the cycles of life, of generations gone by and to come. Immediately the house came to mind and her hand clenched, crumpling the leaves.

"Candy?"

She turned her head as Tina slid into the desk chair next to her. "Hmm?"

"Where'd you go all morning? Michael was looking for you."

"I made a couple of customer calls. Michael say what he wanted?"

Tina shook her head. "No. Have any luck?"

It would take more than luck to figure out Michael, Candy decided. She still was unsure which end was up with him. He was both frustrating and endearing. Half the time she wanted to kill him, and the other half she spent seriously fantasizing about the body under the tight jeans and T-shirts he favored when working on the house. "No," she sighed. "Not really."

"Oh, that's too bad." Tina rolled her shoulders fatalistically. "But not to worry. Something will come up."

That puzzled Candy. "What?"

Tina shrugged. "You'll figure out something to sell to somebody. You'll make club. Time's running short, but there's still a bit left. It's too soon to get all down and depressed over it."

Candy blinked. "Oh. You're talking about my morning sales call."

Cautiously Tina responded, "Yes. I thought that's what we were discussing. You look kind of funny. You okay?"

"Sure, I'm okay."

"Something's on your mind. Come on, give," Tina demanded. "It must be important if it's got your attention

92   HOUSEMATES

in the middle of a workday. What're you brooding about?''

Oh, Lord. Her friend was keying into how much she was distracted of late. She hoped to God Bob hadn't noticed anything. She had to get a grip, remember her priorities—career first. Candy's face turned noncommittal. ''Nothing, really.'' Life, death, the great mandala, nothing too serious or deep. ''Just the house.''

A deep male voice interrupted. ''Hey, Candy, got a minute?''

Candy finished brushing the crumpled leaf bits off her hands and into the trash. She glanced up. ''Hi, Steve. Sure. What do you need?'' Steve was one of the office blond gods. Until a few weeks ago, she'd been eager to date him. She tried to remember what it was she'd found so appealing, but drew a blank.

''I need—''

''Steve,'' Tina interrupted, ''can Candy get back to you in just a bit? We're kind of in the middle of something right now.''

Blond gods were not used to being shut down.

''I only wanted to—''

''Later.'' Tina smiled, but it was the firm kind that brooked no argument.

''You didn't need to send him off,'' Candy said once he'd left. ''I'm not falling apart. Honest, I was thinking about the house, that's all.''

''You have a very odd look,'' Tina insisted. ''What about the house?''

Candy squirmed. ''I don't feel like the real owner. Like it's not really Michael's and mine.''

Tina nodded wisely as she leaned back in her chair and crossed her legs. ''Ah, denial. Your subconscious doesn't want to deal with all the overwhelming details of getting the place back into shape, so it's denying the whole thing exists. Let me reassure you. That horrible mess is all yours.''

Candy smiled slightly as she hauled folders out of her briefcase and set them on her desk. "No, that's not it. At least, I don't think so.'' She shrugged. "It's more the atmosphere inside the house. You can almost hear the ghosts of families past, know what I mean?''

"The way you describe the place, it's so dark and dreary no wonder it seems haunted. Open up the windows and air it out. Get rid of all the heavy Gothic draperies so as much light as possible can get in, then make painting the walls white a top priority. You'll feel much better about it.''

Candy groaned. She would never agree to white walls. They were too sterile for such a beautiful old place. At least Tina had no vote in that. And she didn't know how to describe her feelings on the house any better, either. "It's a family kind of house,'' she stated definitively. "And Michael and I don't qualify. We're impostors and the house knows it.''

Tina looked at her in amazement. "Candy, the house is an inanimate object. It has no feelings.''

Candy disagreed. "There is such an incredible sense of melancholy there. It's overpowering. I'm sure the neighborhood kids sense it, and that's why they think it's haunted. The place is sad, like it's aching for kids to slide down the banister again. Michael and I don't have any to give it.''

"You're being ridiculous,'' Tina stated firmly.

"Am I?''

"Yes. You and Michael are fixing the place up, not for yourselves, but for some as yet unknown family. You're being very unselfish and the house loves you for it.''

94 HOUSEMATES

Candy had to laugh at that. "I'm not so sure the house will love us when we're through. It's a mistake for two such opinionated people to try to share a project like this."

But just let somebody else try to step in and take over. She'd die defending the place, and she rather thought Michael would, as well. "By the time the two of us have reached a compromise on every single job that comes up, the place is going to be a worse disaster than it is now."

"Oh, surely not."

Candy shoved a hand through her hair, pushing it back off her forehead. Then she rested her head on that hand. "And the workmanship, holy smoke. How come men are so totally lacking in fine motor skills? You should see him in action—all gross motor function, very enthusiastic but not very productive. Water goes flying everywhere but on the wall we're washing. Then when he swabs the floor, man, he just redistributes the dirt and tells me not to worry. They're going to be refinished at some point, anyway. Maybe I'm too picky, but honestly, the man's a slob. A well-intentioned one, but a slob nonetheless."

"Welcome to the world of relationships, honey," Tina said with real sympathy in her voice. "We can't live with 'em, and we can't live without 'em. One of life's nasty little tricks, I guess. Better get used to it."

"But we don't have a relationship," Candy complained. "It's not fair."

"Little in life is, sweetie. Little in life is."

Both women jumped as the room reverberated with a loud crash. Candy glanced up, shook up enough to momentarily consider divine intervention in her problems as the source of the noise.

"Sorry," Michael apologized as the two women shivered in the cool draft from the open door. "The door got away from me."

HOUSEMATES

Candy immediately sat straighter in her chair. She smoothed her skirt. Now that she'd spent so much time with him, she was much more aware of Michael as a member of the opposite sex.

Tina snickered as she observed Candy's primping. Candy gave her a dirty look from the corners of her eyes. As far as she was concerned, it was decidedly poor taste to laugh at your best friend when she was all but sunk in an emotional pit of quicksand. Tina could at least *act* sympathetic.

Candy sniffed in the general direction of her friend and turned to Michael. "How are you? All your muscles recovered from the last few days?"

Michael had picked up on her skirt straightening and smoothed his tie in response. "I'm, uh, fine. And yourself?"

"Oh, fine. Just fine." She pushed her hair behind her ear in an unintentionally flirty gesture. "Tina tells me you were looking for me. Anything special you wanted?"

There was no longer any simple answer to that question, he realized. She'd be easy to resist if she'd only stayed two-dimensional. Her wavy blond hair, beautiful blue eyes and fantastic figure would put his niece's fashion doll to shame. Michael could keep himself from falling for a knockout, but looks weren't the only thing Candy had going for her. Unfortunately for him, the more time they spent together, the more he realized there was quite a woman under the blond-bombshell appearance.

He liked her.

But she was a nester, no denying it. Just look at the way she'd insisted on buying those towels. It wasn't even *her* nest, yet she couldn't help feathering it, anyway. He was unsure if Candy was aware of it herself, but she was the kind who'd provide a warm, cozy home for her man. Def-

96   HOUSEMATES

inite marriage material. And he wasn't about to inflict that kind of agony on himself or anyone else he'd come to care for.

He crossed to his own desk and set down his briefcase. Flipping it open, he removed several folders. He brought one over to show Candy and Tina. "I had a few ideas on a difficult sale I'm trying to make. I worked on it over the weekend and between sales calls yesterday and things finally jelled this morning. Thought there might be something you could use, too."

"You worked on office stuff over the weekend?" Candy was flabbergasted. Good grief, she felt a definite inferiority complex coming on. "When? You were with me the whole time."

"You don't exactly use your brain shoveling garbage. There was plenty of time to kick a few ideas around."

"Yes, but..." She'd been drooling over his shoulders and rear every time he leaned over and he'd had nothing more exciting on his mind than number crunching? She was fairly sure she was insulted. She also felt rather small knowing that if the tables had been reversed, if she'd been the one with the terrific sales idea, she probably wouldn't have shared it.

"Actually," Michael began in one of his pathetic attempts at humor that drove his sister crazy, "I found emptying out the first floor and scrubbing it up to be a very cleansing experience."

Candy continued to stare at him while Tina groaned. This was just another in a line of discouraging indications that there was more to Michael than she'd originally thought. She hated this. She did not want to like him, as well as lust after his shoulders.

She only wanted his money, and for only a short period of time. She repeated that to herself.

She hated that he had a sense of humor, as well as a highly developed sense of responsibility and stick-to-it-iveness. And now she knew he was generous, too. He had probably been the kind of kid that mothers loved and kids hated. Frankly, she just wished his sense of responsibility and stick-to-it-iveness were not quite so highly developed. If he didn't relax his pace a bit, she would end up in the hospital, half-dead from trying to keep up with him.

Michael held out the manila folder in his hand. "Look at this," he said. "This is my ticket into Golden Circle five-hundred-percent-of-quota club."

Candy checked the label. "Michael, they just updated year before last."

He nodded. "I know. But I'm going to have to sell something to somebody, so I figure it's worth a shot. Now listen to this and tell me I'm not brilliant." He pulled over another chair, opened the folder and began talking.

Half an hour later, Candy sat back thoughtfully in her chair. Michael watched her expectantly.

It was a funny thing, but when he wore his glasses for close-up work and got so involved in it he let his guard drop, his intellect shone through, along with an endearingly earnest little-boy air. The man had, in fact, a brilliant brain to go with his shoulders and tight butt.

"Michael," she suddenly asked. "Did you get teased a lot when you were a kid?"

He blinked. "I beg your pardon?"

She shrugged. "You're so darn smart and kids can be so mean. I just wondered."

Michael took off his glasses, letting them dangle from his fingers while he rubbed his eyes. What was the woman trying to get at now? He'd been showing her a dynamite sales plan she might be able to implement herself. You'd think she'd be more interested in getting into club than

98 HOUSEMATES

dissecting childhood traumas long past. Women were weird.

"I didn't get very good grades in school," he confessed. "Nobody, including myself, had the slightest inkling I might be bright. Looking back, I think my poor school performance was some kind of subconscious attempt to get my parents to focus on me, instead of on how much they hated each other." He lifted a shoulder negligently. "It didn't work. They divorced and have since gone on to divorce again." And he really didn't like thinking about any of that. It reminded him of how his own future was boxed in by a past he'd had no control over. He thought about it more and more frequently lately. What was it about his family that made them unable to maintain relationships? Oh, hell. He shook his head impatiently. "Let's not get into all that. My childhood wasn't much different from lots of other kids. Now, could we get back to the sales plan?"

Candy arched a brow at his abrupt tone. Obviously Michael did not want to pursue that line of conversation. It might be best to follow his lead. "It's extremely clever," she said sincerely. "Well thought out. You may actually be able to talk them into doing this."

"Yes," he agreed quickly, glad to avoid a dissection of his childhood, "I thought so, too. There are some real benefits for them, the way I've got it set up." He shifted his chair closer and realized immediately that was a mistake. Whatever scent she used was so light it was barely discernible. Still, her womanly essence gently teased his nose, making it difficult to concentrate on the papers in front of him when all he really wanted to do was bury his nose in her hair and hyperventilate. He struggled to stay on track. It was difficult and he cleared his throat.

HOUSEMATES

99

"Remember on Sunday when you mentioned an account you were having a tough sell with?" He gestured to the paperwork on the desk between them. "Wouldn't something like this work there?"

She'd really touched a nerve when she'd asked about his childhood. The frown on his face had been a dead giveaway, along with the impatient way he shoved his glasses back on. The man was unhappy and it was all her fault. She ought to be paying attention to what he was saying. He was right. There were one or two accounts of her own where his plan could work. Instead, all she could think of was that she'd inadvertently brought up unhappy memories for him. "Michael, I put some stew in the slow cooker before I left this morning. You want to stop by for a quick dinner before we go over to the house?"

The words were no sooner out than she regretted them. Not only was it totally unlike her to interrupt a business discussion with an offer of a home-cooked meal, but she suspected it was dangerous, as well. She should not spend any more time than absolutely necessary with Michael, she just knew it.

Michael stared at her, not quite sure what to make of her offer. Candy seemed off balance today. Better not to fight it, he decided.

"Stew would be fine. Now about this sales plan—"

"Six-thirty?"

"Fine. Now about this sales plan—"

"Maybe you'll need more time than that to change."

"No, six-thirty will be fine. Now—"

"Are you thinking about Robeson's Rust-safe for this idea?"

He jumped on that quickly, while he had her attention. "Yes! That's the one. Rust-safe."

100   HOUSEMATES

Candy wrinkled her nose at the mere mention of the company. "Forget it. Gary Felding's in charge over there and he's a real slime-ball. I'm here to tell you I can't even pick the Rust-safe folder out of my file without wanting to go wash my hands."

"He can't be that bad."

"He's worse." Gary Felding had a never-ending supply of polyester handkerchiefs that matched his polyester ties, and he was the only male she knew who still slicked back his hair with a fifties-type greasy hair product. His lubricated head showed the trail blazed by each and every tooth in his comb and had a shine like polished patent leather.

Very different from the way Michael groomed his own head, Candy realized as she gave her handsome colleague an approving glance. Michael's hair was controlled by little more than a daily shampooing and the order imposed by a barber rather than a stylist's sheers. In all the time they'd spent together, she'd never seen him fuss with it. In fact—

Darn, there she went again. Lately, she constantly found herself distracted by thoughts of Michael. It was exceedingly annoying. Only this morning she'd almost walked out of her apartment without unplugging the iron she'd used to press her blouse, all because she'd started thinking about how good he'd looked with a faint sheen of perspiration and an unbuttoned flannel shirt as he worked the wheelbarrow. The flannel shirt had been almost the same color as the blouse she'd been ironing.

She tapped her pencil on Michael's precious plan while she marshaled her thoughts back to the subject at hand— sleazy Gary. "Tell you what," she offered. "I'll take you over there and introduce you to him. You won't believe it until you see it." She rose from her chair, her decision made.

HOUSEMATES

Michael was startled. "Don't you want to call first? Make an appointment?"

"Hey, a good-looking babe like me doesn't need an appointment to see Gary Felding."

Furiously Michael inquired, "You're telling me the guy comes onto you?"

Candy shrugged with a nonchalance she was far from feeling. "I'm telling you it has been spelled out in no uncertain terms that the only way I'll ever get an order from Robeson's Rust-safe is by offering Felding a kickback of a very personal nature."

Michael rose so abruptly his chair skittered back several yards across the carpet. He didn't even glance at it. "I'll kill the jerk."

Candy was surprised by his vehemence. As time had gone by, she'd taken a more philosophical outlook. "Hey, he's his own worst enemy. His company's profits aren't anywhere near where they could be if he'd just update a little bit, and he'll wait for hell to freeze over before I'll offer him anything but a standard contract on the job."

Michael was not about to be placated. Nobody, *nobody* came onto Candy and got away with it. He'd rip off Felding's arm and beat him with it. He'd rip off something a lot more personal and take care of the problem altogether. He'd—

"Michael," Candy said with concern, "your face is turning red. Calm down before you have a stroke. The guy's not worth it. Sooner or later, somebody in upper management's going to notice the slip in profits and fire his rear. I'll slip in then and make a killing."

"That's not going to help you sell your quota this year, though."

Candy shrugged philosophically. "So I don't make club this time. There are worse things in life." My God, was that her talking? If she didn't sell her full quota for the year and make club, her career path would stall. What was she thinking? She had to establish herself now so that later on, when she deemed it time to get married, she could carry her own weight. If her husband took off or became incapacitated the way her own father had, she needed to support herself and any children there might be. That principle had been axiomatic in planning her life since her teens.

Michael, and also Tina, who'd been shamelessly eavesdropping, gaped at her in astonishment. She gave them a wry look. "Forget I said that," she told them as she advised herself to do the same. Touching Michael's arm with one hand, she picked up the Rust-safe file with the other. "Tina, hold down the fort while I pay a call on Gary Felding. I'm going to make club one way or another this year."

Michael covered the hand on his arm with one of his own. "There's only one way you'll be making club with a sale to Rust-safe," he growled. "And that's with me right beside you."

"Do I detect a note of possessive male behavior here?" Tina asked brightly.

"You stay out of this," Michael commanded, not really ready yet to analyze his motivation.

"Club's in Miami this year," Tina warned them both. "I checked. Are you sure this is worth it? Lot of crime down there right now."

"Of course," Candy responded automatically, but was it? She didn't know how she felt about her job anymore. She was too young to be having a mid-life crisis, and flu season was still a month or more away. This was ridiculous. Militantly she straightened her shoulders and prepared herself to do battle with slime-ball Gary. "I can use

HOUSEMATES 103

four all-expense-paid days in the sun as much as the next guy,'' she informed Tina.

And Michael would be there, she reminded herself as she walked out the door with him. Club could be in Alaska in January and she'd still want to go. Besides, she justified righteously, an all-expense-paid vacation constituted the only kind of trip she or Michael would be taking until they unloaded the house, so of course it was worth it.

Torn between laughing, crying and raging, Candy kept quiet on the return trip from their call at Rust-safe.

Before, Gary Felding had never been willing to discuss anything more serious than whether the lipstick Candy favored was flavored or plain. Now, a few more calls and she expected a sale—all because a man had accompanied her.

Euphoria and extreme irritation warred for control of her emotions. She understood the euphoria. If this went through, she'd *exceed* one hundred percent. But she wanted to be irritated with Michael for taking over the call.

Only he hadn't—not really. He'd simply read Gary Felding and known his silent presence wouldn't be enough to get Candy the sale. It would only keep the innuendos to a minimum.

Michael had even apologized to her on the way out to the car. He may have even meant it. It was so hard to tell what a man was thinking.

''So,'' Michael said while she was still trying to decide if she was mad or not. ''We're headed to your place for stew?''

Candy thought about that. Did she still want to provide dinner? It would probably be ungracious to back out now. She *had* issued the invitation, after all, and Michael *had* shared his sales idea with her.

Glancing out the window, she realized they were almost back to the apartment building. "Yeah, I guess."

Michael risked a sideways peek. Not the most gracious acquiescence. She still looked really angry—her mouth was all pinched-looking and the skin right between her brows was in furrows. The proper course to take here escaped him. Should he go into an impassioned defense of what he'd done? She'd yet to really accuse him of anything.

Was he to assume she understood he'd done it for her? Club wouldn't be much fun without her there to tease. And although he was smart enough not to say so out loud, it satisfied the male in him to be able to handle this for her.

"Wonder what all the sirens are," he commented casually as they got to within a few blocks of dinner. God, he was hungry. Mostly for Candy, but right about now the stew wouldn't go wasted, either. "You want to stop for a loaf of French bread or something?"

You know, there *were* an awful lot of sirens. "No. I thought I'd toss in some dumplings and let them cook while we made some salad."

"Fine, I'll— My God, that's *our* block that's cordoned off. Look at all the fire trucks!"

Anxiously Candy peered through the windshield. "Pull into that spot over there, Michael," she said, pointing to a tiny space between two parked cars. "I've got a bad feeling about this."

"Me, too," Michael murmured as he jockeyed back and forth, forcing the car into the small spot. Finally they were free to run to the barricades. "See anything?" he asked her as they craned their necks around the throng of spectators.

"No," Candy admitted in frustration. "But look at all the smoke! Everyone's pointing down to the end of the block where our building is." Frantically she glanced

HOUSEMATES

around. "Officer! Excuse me, but can you tell me which building is burning?"

The policeman looked around, located Candy and informed her, "Second building from the corner, down on the left."

"Oh, my God," Candy responded weakly as Michael stared grimly down the street. Second building from the corner. That was their building.

The policeman scratched his head and yelled at a teenager trying to duck under the barricade on a dare. "Hey, you, get back. Try that again and I'll haul you out of here in the back of a squad car, hear me?" Satisfied he'd made his point, the cop turned back to Michael and Candy. "Seems to have started in the front of the building. Once it got in the walls—" He shook his head. "Nobody'll be sleeping there tonight," he predicted. "That place is history."

The officer continued conversationally, "Be interesting to find out what caused this. One of my cousins used to have one of those slow cookers, I remember. Started a batch of stew before she left for the day once and the cord shorted out while she was gone. Came home to a pile of ash."

Candy's eyes widened, then returned to normal. "He said the front of the building," she mouthed to Michael. "I'm in the back."

"My wife uses one of those curling-iron things," the officer went on. "Now those babies really get hot. Don't know why the emergency room doesn't see a lot more women with fried scalps. If it's left near a towel, or bathroom curtains, well . . ." He left the rest unsaid.

Candy smiled a bit sickly. She needed to get out of there. "Thank you, officer." She turned and began edging her way back through the crowd. No point worrying about the

106 HOUSEMATES

stew now. Nine would get you ten it was overdone, to say the least.

"I don't believe this," Michael hissed as he followed in her wake. "How can you look so calm? Everything you own is currently polluting the sky. Hell, everything *I* own is currently polluting the sky."

"Let's not jump to any hasty conclusions." Candy stopped moving once she reached the fringe of the group of spectators. She spoke to herself, as well as Michael. "Maybe they'll be able to salvage some of our things." Man, she sure hoped. Her champagne towels with the lace trim were there in a bag on her closet shelf. She hadn't even removed the price tags yet. Forlornly she watched smoke curl ponderously upward as though reluctant to leave, preferring to hang heavily along the ground stinging their eyes and burning their noses as a reminder of all it was taking.

Cold seeped through her coat, making her shiver. "Michael?" she called miserably.

"Right here, babe," he answered from just behind her, making an attempt to cool down. If yelling could change things, his father's life would have changed course many a time. He placed his hands on her shoulders and, when he felt her trembling, pulled her back against him. Encircling her with his arms, he rested his chin on the top of her hair.

"Those beautiful towels I bought..."

He supposed it would be crass to point out he'd never wanted them in the first place. "Forget it, sugar," he told her. "They're carbon by now."

She sniffed. She couldn't help it. "They were so perfect. Just what I wanted in there."

"Yeah, well, try to put things in perspective. They're the least of your worries. All your good work clothes are gone,

HOUSEMATES

your casual stuff, your furniture, CD player, television, all your memories, the photo albums, college and high school yearbooks, everything you cared about is gone.'' And so was his. Dammit, anyway.

"Thanks, Michael, that really helped. What are we going to do?'' She leaned back against him and tried to think. The shock of knowing her every possession was burned to a crisp, combined with the nearness of Michael's body, rendered the task near impossible.

"I don't know, Candy. I just don't know.'' Why now? he wondered. The timing couldn't have been worse. Neither one of them had much cash to replace anything. It was all tied up in the house, and who knew how long it would take the insurance company to come through? He blew out a great pent-up lungful of air. "Come on, let's get out of here.''

"Where are we going?'' she asked as she reluctantly allowed herself to be tugged away from the mesmerizing sight.

"The Salvation Army before they close. We need clothes to work at the house in. I'm not paying full price for that kind of stuff.''

"Okay,'' Candy agreed, amazed he could think at all right then.

"I hope you've got some stuff at the cleaner's,'' Michael growled. "I dropped off some suits and a few shirts a couple of days ago. That'll hold me for a while. We'll stop there, too, then go to the mall and get whatever we need to set up housekeeping at the house.''

"We're staying overnight there?'' Candy asked, amazed to find herself breathless at the implications.

"It's better than running up a hotel bill, don't you think?'' he asked as he stuffed her into the car and came around to his side. He began working the car out of the tight spot he'd sandwiched it into. "Lord only knows how long it will take the insurance money to come through. Even then, we won't get replacement value. I'll bet anything they'll take what we originally paid for our things, then devalue them for the number of years we've owned them and give us that price." He left unspoken that it would take years to recover from such a disaster unless they made an awful lot of money on the sale of the house. Candy could figure that out for herself.

Her mind reeled. Out of everything pressing down on her right then, her mind seemed fixated on staying overnight at the house with Michael. She didn't know how she felt about that. If they stayed overnight in the house together, would he try anything? Did she want him to try anything? Oh, Lord.

Chapter Seven

After they'd gone their separate ways at the mall, Candy realized she had no idea what to expect that night in terms of sleeping arrangements. She didn't want Michael to think she was inviting a pass, yet if he should happen to think of it on his own, she'd rather not be running around the house in heavy flannels with feet in the bottom.

She took a 360-degree turn in the center of the lingerie area. Negligees were out—too blatant. Besides, the house would be cool. The weather lately displayed all the typical neurotic tendencies of midautumn. The days warmed up beautifully, but the evenings and nights brought on the shivers. It was October, after all.

Her eyes roamed to the next rack. College dorm T-shirt nighties with matching socks wouldn't make the grade, either. Too, well . . . too collegiate.

She needed to hurry. Michael would be wondering— There! "Perfect," she breathed as she stopped in front of a rack of satin floor-length night wear. Feminine, but not

110 HOUSEMATES

blatant about it, the satin had a brushed-flannel backing that also ensured warmth. She bought one and added it to her stack of parcels.

"Candy," Michael called as soon as he saw her headed his way. "Over here. What kept you?"

"Oh, have you been waiting long? I must have misunderstood. I thought you said meet at the escalator at six-thirty," Candy said, lying without compunction. "I thought I had ten minutes left."

Michael gave her a disbelieving look, then took her arm and steered her onto the escalator. He ended up standing uncomfortably in the middle of the linen-display area feeling decidedly like a male drowning in a sea of feminine lace-trimmed flowers and sachets. Candy was already exclaiming over a set of towels that reminded him of the set that had been offered to Vulcan, god of fire, only that afternoon.

"Cheap," he hissed at her. "All we want is a couple of inexpensive towels and a cheap set of sheets."

Candy's eyes lifted from the beautiful linens and met his. "That's something we need to talk about, Michael," she began determinedly. "We haven't discussed sleeping arrangements. Now, I notice you said *a* cheap set, as in singular. Now, (a) that's a contradiction in terms—there's no such thing as a cheap set of sheets, and (b) exactly what did you have in mind here? Where, precisely, did you plan for us to put our heads down for the night?"

Michael had the grace to redden slightly. She was right. They should have talked this over. "Well, I thought we'd buy a double mattress, a set of sheets and a blanket. You don't have to worry about my attacking you, if that's your concern. I'm quite capable of controlling myself when the need arises. You can always put a board or something down the center of the bed if it'll make you feel better," he

HOUSEMATES

offered. "I'm just trying to come up with the most economical plan of action here. Two mattresses and box springs would be expensive, and we'd have to buy twin-bed frames, as well. But there is that old double frame we found up in one of the bedrooms, remember? We can use that. Now come on. Help me look. There must be a set of plain white sheets here someplace." He glanced helplessly around.

Candy studied him with narrowed eyes as he began to wander down an aisle. She'd never have believed that line from anybody else. With Michael, however, it was a real possibility he was telling the truth. It was possible he had no ulterior motives. The man was cheap.

She followed him. "Listen, Michael, why don't we just grab some towels and find a couple of camp cots somewhere?"

Camp cots, was she kidding? Did he look like Paul Bunyan? He'd hated camp as a kid. Heck, the last time he'd slept on a camp cot, he'd come home to find his parents living at two separate addresses. To make the transition easier for him, they'd said. What a laugh. He'd never even stayed overnight at a friend's after that; God only knew what would have been cooked up while he was gone.

He snorted. "No camp cots. We're in this for a lot more than one night, you know. Our backs would be broken after the first night. That old bedstead in the back bedroom is our best bet."

Candy wasn't so sure. Even the best of intentions could go by the wayside if they were pushed hard enough. "I don't know, Michael . . ."

Michael gritted his teeth. She'd been through a lot today. Maybe something other than white would make her happier. He'd unbend a little, although not to the point where he found himself sleeping in a flower bower. He

112   HOUSEMATES

glanced around, then strode determinedly to a shelving unit neatly stacked with solid-color sheets.

"Look." He pointed to a plastic-wrapped blue set on the shelf. "Any color sheets you could want. Pick one. Blue, red, whatever. Your choice." He inspected the price code. "Five dollars more than plain white, but I guess they're worth it." He smiled at her, feeling terribly magnanimous.

Candy looked from him to the sheets and back to him. "You don't think it would be worth it to splurge on that gorgeous set over there?" she asked carefully, wistfully. "And you have to agree to wear pajamas. At least the bottoms. And swear you'll stay on your own side. All night."

He smiled placatingly. "All right, I swear I'll wear bottoms and stay on my own side, but I simply cannot deal with flowers and lace on my bed. I'm sorry, but I can't." He sighed. Hell. A fancy pair of sheets was nothing compared to the cost of an extra bed frame, mattress and box spring. Further compromising seemed in order. "Okay, how about that set over there? I could live with red-and-blue plaid."

She shook her head. "It's so masculine," she protested.

Well, he was, too, or had she really not noticed?

She turned in a slow circle. "Um, let's see..." Lace, ruffles, more lace. "There. How's that. A beautiful, rich blue, green and purple paisley and floral combination."

"There are flowers all over it," Michael complained.

"Just a few overlying the paisley," she said. "It's a good compromise for us."

Flowers and a high price tag was a compromise? Oh, hell. Candy had more stamina than he did. She might look

HOUSEMATES 113

dead on her feet, but he doubted she ever got too tired to argue. "Fine. Do it."

Candy was pleased when Michael gave the okay to buy the sheets. She'd expected more of an argument over both the flowers and the price, but she was becoming more and more impressed with Michael's handling of the current crisis. It had taken him all of ten minutes to come to grips with the fact he'd just lost everything he owned and set in motion a plan to cope with the situation. A man who maintained control under pressure was something special, she acknowledged.

She, on the other hand, was exhausted, both emotionally and physically. She'd pay any price, she decided, if she could just talk somebody into delivering a chair, with a hassock to put her feet up on, to the house sometime in the next twenty minutes.

Instead, they picked up a card table and folding chairs for the dining room, then Michael dragged her to a mattress warehouse. Even there a box spring and mattress set them back a bundle. Candy watched while Michael supervised the knotting of the ropes holding them to the top of the car.

"Are you sure you want a mismatched set?" she asked one more time.

Michael never took his eyes off the knotting procedure. "Candy, we went through all this. The guy gave us fifty dollars off on a good-quality mattress and spring just because they were two oddballs he had left over."

"But the designs on them don't match," Candy wailed. Damn. She was setting up housekeeping, sort of, for the first time with a man. Everything should be perfect. She'd scheduled her life, worked hard and long, aiming for this moment, and look—their new mattress was pink and sat-

114   HOUSEMATES

iny while the box spring was off-white with purple flowers on the sides.

"Candy, be reasonable," Michael responded in what he hoped was a calm manner. "We bought nice sheets, a good blanket and a matching spread. The spread's the only thing that's going to show when the bed's made. The spring and mattress are buried so far down under all those layers you and I are the only ones who will ever know they don't match. We need that money for other stuff."

"I know, I know." And she did. Of course he was right. But she was still upset. She attempted to rein in her runaway emotions. All in all, it had been a hell of a day. "I need to relax with a glass of wine," she told him.

Michael was a gem, she decided forty-five minutes later. He had to be as tired as she was, but he'd stopped at a twenty-four-hour convenience store and run in. When he emerged five minutes later, he had a bottle of decent-quality wine, some cheese and a box of scallop-edged crackers. She hadn't even had to remind him.

"We'll light a fire in the living-room fireplace," he told her as he climbed back into the car. "Our first one. It'll be nice to unwind in front of the flames with a glass of rosé." They deserved it after what they'd been through. He was feeling close to Candy right then. Some shrink would probably say they'd been through a bonding experience or some such nonsense. Whatever it was, he felt it and wanted to share some downtime with her. Nothing too exotic. Just sit together in front of a fire. Maybe put his arm around her. Maybe share a kiss or two. He was exhausted but, man, the idea appealed.

"To tell you the truth, Michael, the last thing I feel like doing right now is lighting a fire. I've seen enough flames today to last me a lifetime. I may never toast another marshmallow in my life. Let's just have a quick glass in the kitchen and go to bed. Maybe we'll wake up in the morning and discover this day never happened—that it was all just a bad dream.'' Besides, relaxing with Michael did not seem like a prudent choice to her. Her guard was down tonight, and frankly it would probably be a whole lot better to avoid the type of scenario Michael was painting.

The corners of Michael's mouth drooped with disappointment. Now that he thought about it, he supposed it was reasonable that Candy wouldn't want to gaze into a fire with him. As she'd pointed out, they'd done enough of that this afternoon. But damn, he needed to relax a bit, and for reasons best left unexamined, he'd wanted to do it with her.

Oh, well. It was probably for the best. A man could get into trouble with the scene he'd just envisioned. ''You're probably right.'' He sighed. ''We've still got to wrestle the mattress and box spring up to the second floor and set up all the rest of this stuff. I guess we'd better get to it as quickly as we can. We'll be up half the night as it is.''

The house was hidden sullenly behind the front-yard pines as Michael pulled onto the two narrow ribbons of broken concrete that posed as a driveway.

''I don't think it wants us here,'' Candy announced judiciously as she studied the front facade.

''Tough. It's got us.'' Michael grunted as he got out of the car and began slicing through the ropes holding the mattress and springs to the car roof.

Candy shivered. ''Look how dark and unwelcoming it is.''

''So we'll turn on a few lights. Remind me to buy a couple of spots for the front area. And a timer.''

So pragmatic. So logical. She could learn to hate him.

116 HOUSEMATES

"Get ready to catch this thing. I'm going to start pushing it off now."

Candy's eyes widened in alarm. "No, wait!"

Michael turned back and spoke with exaggerated patience. "What now? Listen, Candy, can it wait until we're inside? It's freezing out here."

"I just want us to think about this a little more. I doubt I can catch something that big and heavy."

"Then just slow its fall. Okay, here it comes."

"I think it would be better if we both pulled, rather than you pushing it at me. Or let me push and you catch. Oh, my God, Michael! I can't hold it! I'm dropping it!"

"I'm coming. I'm coming. Hang on one more second." Michael raced around the car barely in time to rescue a red-faced straining Candy as she unsuccessfully juggled the wobbly mattress.

"Michael," she gasped as she tried to catch her breath once the mattress was on the ground and leaning against the car, "I asked you to wait."

"It's the difference between taking half an hour to slowly peel a bandage off and just ripping the thing off. Instead of debating the best method to do the job half the night, look, it's done. Now, which side do you want?"

Candy narrowed her eyes. She was quite sure Michael sincerely felt the end had justified the means. She, however, had been the one almost buried alive under God knew how many pounds of suffocating mattress. It wouldn't take much to prod her into pointing that little fact out. "Michael..."

"What?" He was busily surveying the listing box spring still clinging precariously to the top of the car.

She took a deep breath, remembering the rules for arguing they'd set up. Michael had followed them—most of the evening. They were both overtired, she reminded her-

HOUSEMATES 117

self. Instead of letting him have it, she counted slowly to ten.

"Candy—"

"That side." She pointed to the edge nearest her own position. "I want to go up the stairs first. You can be the one pushing from below. I'll pull."

"Thanks a bunch."

Candy shrugged. "Hey, it's a medical fact. Women don't have the upper body strength that men have. They're put together differently."

He'd noticed. He especially noticed the way Candy was put together. Maybe it was a good thing she was too tired for a fire.

"All right, on the count of three . . ."

Michael didn't argue as Candy took control. He just wanted to get the thing inside.

It took some doing, but gradually they approached their goal.

"Candy, you've got to hold your end up higher."

"I can't. This is as high as I can manage. Be careful. You're going to hit the light fixture."

"I can't see where it is. The mattress is blocking— Oh."

Candy sighed as glass showered down. "Well, at least it's just the globe. We still have light. Don't cut yourself."

"We're both wearing shoes. We'll be fine."

Yeah, gym shoes. She sighed quietly on her side of the mattress. She'd just step carefully.

"Okay, let's do it. Lift."

She lifted. Michael pushed. She pulled. They both swore, although Michael was far more inventive.

They rested on the landing and tried to catch their breaths before struggling onward. When they finally reached their goal, they immediately turned around and went back for the spring. It was after midnight before the bedstead left behind by the previous owners had been wiped clean and assembled. They built their bower right in the middle of the room, so they wouldn't have to move it when it came time to repair and paint the walls.

Candy cleaned the bathroom and prayed the bulge in the ceiling wouldn't let loose while one of them was using it. Michael fought with the sheets until they surrendered and lay sulkily across the bed. He added the royal-blue blanket Candy had picked to coordinate with the paisley sheets. Then, as carefully as if it had been gold—and that was about how it had been priced—he smoothed out the matching bedspread.

He stepped back after plumping the pillows into position and gazed at his masterpiece. There were a few lumps he hadn't quite managed to tame, but all in all, it looked pretty damn good.

He eyed it from another angle. Candy had a good eye for color, he'd give her that. Maybe, when this whole fiasco was over, he'd give her the whole bed set, as a sort of remembrance of their time together. Nodding, he said to no one in particular, "She's been a good sport about this whole mess." He'd have gone nuts if she'd fallen apart and cried all afternoon, instead of pitching in, he acknowledged. "She deserves it."

"You say something, Michael?"

"What? Oh, no, nothing. Just talking to myself."

"Oh, well, I'm almost done in here. Do you mind if I shower first?"

"Sure, if you can get it to work. You may have to take a bath, instead."

"Whatever. Right now I'll take what I can get. Would you mind finding me a towel out of whatever bag it's in, some soap from wherever that is and the sack from Marshall's?"

HOUSEMATES 119

"Sure." He checked the cache from the mall. It lay in a great pile along one wall of the bedroom. Sighing, he began the search. The fifth bag yielded the toiletries, and he pulled out a new toothbrush, toothpaste and soap. He discovered her new nightie in the Marshall's bag and put it over one arm. It felt like silk. At the thought of possibly holding her once she had it on, his exhausted body hardened. He'd never be able to keep his word to her at this rate. He'd have to be very careful not to look directly at her once she had the thing on, that was all.

Last, he located the linen bag. He pulled out a plain beige bath towel. It really was a shame the ones Candy had loved so had been burned before she'd ever even clipped off the tags. He tried to remember if she'd ever mentioned her birthday as he carried his finds to where she stood at the bathroom door. Would a woman find a gift of towels romantic or insulting?

"Here you are. Nice nightgown." He let it go reluctantly.

She looked at him uncertainly. "Thanks." The satin visibly sparked as she took it from him. The air in the house must be dry. Must be static electricity.

"You're welcome." He stood there with his hands in his pockets just looking at her. Must be something to that bonding-experience stuff. Look at her. Ruffled and flustered as she was, she still turned him inside out. Man, he was in trouble. Buying only one mattress and box spring may have been a bad idea. The idea of camp cots was starting to look good.

"Listen," he said, "you take your time. I'm going to tack up some of the drop cloths over the bedroom windows and then I think I'll bring up the portable TV we brought in last weekend. I completely forgot about the fourth game in the World Series being on tonight." Imagine forgetting something of that magnitude. That alone told him how upset the house, the fire and Candy had him. "They're out on the West Coast. I might be able to catch the last couple of innings. You just . . . take your time." Please. He desperately needed to cool down.

He had the drop cloths tacked up before he heard the water start running. His imagination cranked itself into high gear as he imagined her preparing for the tub. It was a good thing they hadn't indulged in the wine after all. He was in bad enough shape. Sweat broke out on his forehead. Swearing, he strode down the steps and retrieved the small portable TV. Thank God the fire hadn't gotten that. There wasn't a man alive who couldn't lose himself in a good baseball game. It might even work for him tonight.

The shower functioned. Candy tested it, then decided to take a bath, anyway. It was a delaying tactic. But she still wasn't sure what to expect once she hit the bedroom, so delaying tactics seemed appropriate.

Candy made the water good and hot. The steam served to warm the chilly room, and she hoped the heat of the water would soothe her jangled nerves. Stepping into the tub, she slid down low, letting the water engulf her body up to her chin. Then she tried to think. It wasn't easy.

She wondered if Michael was out there looking for a board. He'd promised to stay on his own side—all night. Michael, she'd learned, was one of those men whose word was his bond. He'd do it. So why had she felt that niggling bit of disappointment when he'd so readily agreed to her bedroom rules?

Her brow furrowed as she soaped her arm. What if she released him from his bond? What then? Immediately her skin broke out in goose bumps. Drat. Hurriedly she submerged her arm again as she strangled the soap in one fist.

HOUSEMATES

She sat up again, shivering as the cooler air hit her damp heated body. Once more she applied herself to soaping. This time, she took care of her chest. Never had her breasts reacted so violently to a lousy washing. But the full flesh-covered mounds were so sensitized tonight she was aware of each minuscule soap bubble popping. She tried to get herself back under control, but the soap swirling around her breasts and over her puckering nipples was a constant reminder of what might—or might not—be waiting to happen in the other room.

"This is ridiculous," she muttered out loud as she sank back below the water, determinedly rinsing all the suds off. She half expected to see steam rise from the tub as she submerged. Moments later, she pulled the plug and stepped out onto the floor. "I'm a full-grown woman," she grumbled to a mirror so fogged over there wasn't even the slightest reflection. "What do I want to happen here tonight?"

Taking a corner of the towel she'd wrapped around herself, she swiped it over the mirror, clearing the center portion. Then she pasted a determined look on her face and checked it in the reflective surface, making sure she wore it firmly. "A mature woman," she lectured herself, "is capable of making these types of decisions. Now, do I choose to sleep with him—in the biblical sense, that is, for after all, I'll be literally sleeping with him regardless—or not?"

That said, she glared at her reflection.

Well? Did she want to *sleep* with him or simply sleep with him?

She loaded her toothbrush, then jammed it into her mouth. Instantly her lips foamed pale blue as she scrubbed.

Well?

She pulled her nightgown over her head. It hung stiffly from her still-aching and pointed breasts. Her hair was brushed, the towel hanging over the shower curtain rod and her toothbrush in the freshly scrubbed-out medicine cabinet, along with the neatly recapped toothpaste.

Well?

Slowly, she nodded at herself in the mirror. You know, she really rather thought she did want to sleep with him. Michael was one of the good guys. That had been clear all along. But her reasoning went deeper than that. She'd never given herself to a man before. Michael would be the first, and she'd met plenty of other good guys wandering through her life.

No, it was more than that. There was an underlying sensual pull and sense of rightness about this that must have been there all along. That had to be why she'd overreacted to his last name. Even now, she couldn't help snorting. Michael Cane. Candy Cane. No way. It really was too bad it had to feel so right with a man with such an awful name.

But maybe, just maybe there was the barest possibility, the teensiest tiniest chance, that she was falling in love here, and that was why everything was clicking into place tonight. After all, she'd turned down guys before. There was something about Michael that was so irresistibly...right. "Bummer," she muttered as she gave her reflection one final check in the mirror before the glass misted over again.

Still, there was no denying the inevitability of the evening's direction. She was going to do it. For the first time in her life, she really was.

She opened the bathroom door. She entered the bedroom. She—

Michael was asleep.

HOUSEMATES 123

Look at him. Sprawled on top of the blanket, he'd at least thought to turn down the new spread and kick off his shoes. Hands on her hips, foot tapping, she studied him through narrowed eyes. This was unbelievable. After everything she'd just struggled with in the bathroom, reaching the single most important decision of a woman's life, and the lucky guy fell asleep? She didn't know if she should laugh or cry.

She sighed as Michael's foot twitched in his sleep. He must have turned off the overhead light when he'd lain down to watch the game. The television provided the only illumination in the room. The low light flickered over Michael's face, throwing deep shadows that added extra strength to his features. It caught in his dark hair and played there, moving with him when he twisted restlessly in his sleep.

He looked good. Darn good.

Life can be so unfair, she thought as she flicked off the TV. If he'd been watching a baseball game, it was over. She wondered if Michael knew who'd won or why he'd even care. It wasn't as if a Chicago team was involved in the World Series this year. But that was a man for you. Sports, the male sex substitute. She glared at the darkened bed. Nothing moved. Reluctantly she started toward it. A double bed wasn't all that wide, she realized. Especially when an inert male form was sprawled across two-thirds of it. She should wake him up. He'd want to brush his teeth, clean up a bit, kiss her good-night. Oh, good grief. She'd never acted in such a depraved manner before. What was wrong with her? Leave the poor man alone, for heaven's sake.

Gingerly she lifted a corner of the sheet and blanket, then slid in, holding her breath. But there was no change in Michael, not even a hitch in his breathing. Turning her back to him, Candy clung to the edge of the bed and tried to sleep.

She sat up fifteen minutes later and carefully pulled the spread over Michael. It was cold in the house, and she didn't want him catching a chill. Not that he didn't deserve to. She was still annoyed with him for falling asleep while she'd struggled with her conscience and other assorted personal demons.

Lying back down, she cautiously wriggled back against him. She'd eaten the same food he had today, otherwise she'd swear he was drugged, he was out so cold. Well, it allowed her to take advantage of his body warmth without feeling wanton. She'd totally changed her mind about sleeping with him, but it was darn cold in this house. Maybe tomorrow they'd tackle the old furnace, try to coax a few days' heat out of it until the new one was ready.

Thoughts of all that needed doing tomorrow exhausted her, and with Michael beside her, warming her, it wasn't long before she felt herself being sucked down into slumber.

Michael awoke with a start and a sense of disorientation. Where was he? This wasn't his futon. Why was it so dark? Ever since he'd tripped over his briefcase in the dark one evening and broken a toe, he'd always left a light on in the bathroom.

Panicked, he sat up. Who the hell was in the bed with him? He didn't even remember being with a woman. He hadn't even been *interested* in another woman since meeting that maddening confection named Candy Barr.

His eyes widened as memory flooded back. Oh, God, it was Candy. She'd been in the bathroom. He'd been watching the game. He dragged a hand through his hair. He must have fallen asleep. Had the Padres won or lost?

HOUSEMATES

What a stupid question to ask when Candy was asleep beside him in that satiny nightie he'd handed her at the bathroom door. My God, she was beautiful. And he was a Sox fan, anyway.

He wiped a hand over his face as his heart began to slow down again. He studied the form curled next to him. Candy lay on her side, her pillow tucked neatly under her head, blond hair fanned beguilingly over the brightly patterned case. With a start, he realized the sheets they'd "compromised" on complemented her coloring perfectly. "Couldn't be more effective if she planned it," he said aloud, then regretted the disruptive sound in the dark and quiet cocoon they'd created in the bed.

Candy lay there so trustingly, looking so young and innocent. Had she been disappointed or relieved to find him asleep? His eyes narrowed. Or had she been indifferent? Her back was to him. Had that been by design or happenstance? Something about this situation reminded him of a sitcom—the married man trying to figure out if his wife was speaking to him or not. The thought filled him with a hitherto unknown longing—and an odd depression that those concerns would never be his.

Frustrated and reluctant, he peeled back the spread and slowly climbed out of bed. Goose bumps immediately broke out on his arms as the chilled air hit him. "Candy must have covered me," he realized as he hurried into the bathroom. "She must care, at least a little." He turned on the shower, pulled off his Salvation Army jeans and sweatshirt, and stepped under the anemic spray, feeling slightly better.

Chapter Eight

Fifteen minutes later, Michael was back by the side of the bed. Bare-chested, his hair still damp from the shower, he stood looking down at Candy. He'd donned pajama bottoms as a concession to Candy and the cold house. And also as an additional barrier, however flimsy, to remind himself that while they might have the appearance of a normal married couple at home, they were anything but. Sex with Candy meant commitment. She wasn't ready for it, and when she was, he still wasn't the right man.

He pulled back the top sheet and blanket, then carefully eased himself into the bed. Immediately a violent shiver took him. Damn, percale must be a code name for spun ice.

He held his breath as Candy rolled over to face him.

One eye opened groggily. "Michael? What's the matter? Are you sick?"

"No, I'm fine," he whispered, his voice reflecting the influence of the surrounding quiet darkness. Go back to

HOUSEMATES 127

sleep, he silently urged. I'm hanging on to my good intentions by a thread. Whatever you do, don't start wriggling around in the bed. To his great relief, her eye drifted shut again.

Life in the suburbs certainly differed from life in the city, he reflected as he lay there, unable to relax. If he strained, he could hear a dog barking. But that was way off in the distance somewhere. That sporadic sound constituted the only noise he could hear. He concentrated on it—anything to distract him and keep him from reaching over, grabbing Candy and scaring the pants off her. Then he found himself wondering if she even *had* panties on under that satin nightie. "Oh, God," he groaned.

Both her eyes popped open. A note of alarm entered her voice. "You *are* sick!"

He was in pain, that was what he was. Deep physical pain. "I'm not sick," he got out through gritted teeth. At least not the way she meant. He was in an agony of need. God, what he'd give to reach out to her, slide his hand up her thigh and satisfy his curiosity. He shook harder, and the cool sheets had little to do with the problem.

"Then why are you shaking like that?"

"The bed got cold while I was showering," Michael complained while he tried to control himself. "I'm sorry I woke you."

Candy's laugh was light with relief. "Oh, is that all? Here, come here, and I'll warm you up."

Michael froze in place. Was she serious? She'd do that? His sister had put her cold feet on him once as a joke and he'd practically jumped a mile. Candy must be a saint, and he was struggling not to be a sinner. Slowly he turned on his side to face her.

She fitted her body against his, steeling herself against the invading chill she was immediately subject to. She wrapped her arms around his shoulders and held him tightly. She'd give him just a taste of what he'd missed by falling asleep, she decided. That would teach him.

She was plastered against him and Michael's breath backed up in his lungs, finally escaping with a whoosh. His arms closed convulsively around her and he stuck his nose in her neck. Damn, she smelled good, all female and soft, and the satin of her gown rubbed against his chest in a manner so erotic a man could die from it.

But hey, if your time's up, there are worse ways to go, he decided.

He fought to keep his hands from roving, but he couldn't refrain from nuzzling her neck. He let his tongue sneak a quick taste and found a hint of coconut, a whisper of strawberry. If only he was the happily-ever-after type, he thought as he battled against the urge to take a second lick, he'd go quite happily to his doom. Heck, even knowing his odds against a successful union, the urge to try something stupid along those lines with the delectable piece of confection beside him was amazingly strong.

It mightn't hurt too much to just sort of massage her back a bit. He couldn't do a terrific job of it, having to reach around her the way he would, but her muscles were probably stiff after their rough day and she'd probably appreciate whatever effort he made. And of course, holding her close and rubbing up against her satin-clad body so he could reach her back more easily would be more in the line of a corporal work of mercy for him. Certainly not a cheap thrill.

Awkwardly, and irritated with that awkwardness, he moved his hand. God, she was soft. He wrapped his leg around her and kneaded a bit harder. He'd yet to find any knots. She was supple and smooth beneath his hands.

"Michael?"

HOUSEMATES

129

"Hmm?" he murmured as he inhaled deeply of her unique fragrance.

"Thanks. That feels good."

"Yes, it does. I mean, uh, I'm glad. You're welcome." Could she feel what her nearness was doing to him? How could she not? His body was not being precisely subtle in its reaction. He'd have to stop soon.

Candy's senses were rapidly becoming swamped. Michael's crisp chest hair prickled her right through her nightgown. He'd warmed up nicely, too, although his hair was still damp from his shower. She needed to stay close a bit longer, she decided. No point in Michael's getting ill from taking a chill. Not when she was right there to prevent it.

Where did the man hide these shoulders when he put on a suit? she wondered once again as she rubbed circles along their width with two palms. This was incredible. Absolutely incredible. Muscled and broad, they were lightly covered with hair, which tickled her palms as she traced her way from his shoulders down the length of his thick arms.

She leaned back a bit and studied his face. "You know," she murmured, "without your glasses, you look so different. Not that you don't look good when you come into the office—you do—but it's like you're wearing camouflage or something. The Clark Kent syndrome. Your suit and glasses hide something." How about pure, unadulterated animal magnetism? "I don't know what it is, but no one in the office would recognize you right now."

Michael thought about the rather compromising position they were in and responded with gratitude. "Thank God for that," he murmured.

"What did you say, Michael?" Candy asked as she placed a kiss with all the weight of a butterfly on the strong slash of collarbone at the base of his neck.

130 HOUSEMATES

Michael sucked in his breath. "Nothing, honey. Absolutely nothing." Then he kissed her, full on the lips, and it was anything but lightweight.

Candy kissed him back without hesitation. He wanted her. The burgeoning bulge against her stomach was silent witness to his need, but she wasn't afraid. This was Michael and she was sure of what came next. It would be right for her—right for them. As she sunk under the powerful spell of the kiss, she decided living your life on some kind of rigid time schedule was ludicrous. This was her life and she was in love *now*.

The realization stunned her. It had happened. To her. It had to be love. Candy Cane was sounding awfully good to her right then, but she ruthlessly shut off that line of thought. She might be ready to entertain fantasies of having kids and maybe even keeping this house to raise them in, but she knew Michael wasn't. Suddenly she was impatient with all the obstacles she sensed in their way and became even more determined to show Michael what he'd be missing.

His hand was easing up her nightie now. Oh, Lord, here we go, she thought.

Her legs were like satin. Smooth but supple. She was exquisite, and he found himself breathing deeply in an effort to feed his laboring lungs some much needed oxygen.

Letting his hand glide up the back of her thigh, he quickly found the swell of her sweet buttock. She shivered. "You're chilly," he said regretfully. "I've made you cold."

"No! No, I'm not. Really." Actually she was hot, getting hotter every second. She just might have to strip off her nightgown any second to cool herself down a bit. Then again, Michael might take care of the problem for her. He had it up over her hips now. One of his hands cupped her

HOUSEMATES

buttock while he'd let the other slide to the front of her body.

She tensed as he let it drift around her stomach and then meander up her rib cage. Her breath caught as his hand stalled out just beneath her breast. The backs of his fingers rubbed back and forth along the lower swell as he hesitated.

She couldn't stand it. She took his hand in hers and moved it up so that he cupped her. It was heaven. "Michael, kiss me. Please?"

"Oh, God, yes." She wanted him. Wasn't she practically pleading with him to go on? All his hesitation fled. He held her tight, his arousal close against her. This moment alone was worth all the aggravation and uncertainty of the past few months. It was worth the upheaval of the move and having his apartment building burn down.

As his lips touched hers, they felt singed and he could feel heat. The kiss rapidly blew out of control. He wanted to devour her mouth. He wanted to devour *her*.

"What the hell?" Michael hung on to Candy as a loud crack sounded in the room and the bed dropped out from under them.

"Oh, my God! Michael, what's happening?"

"Damned if I know. Hold on a second."

She clung to him. "Believe me, I'm not going anywhere."

Michael cradled Candy to him with one arm while he fought his way free of the sheets and blankets with the other. The mattress and spring lay tilted crazily at a forty-five-degree angle down the frame, and Michael and Candy fought to keep from being dumped on the floor.

Finally Michael scrambled free of the disaster and helped Candy to her feet.

"What do you think happened?" she whispered as she pushed hair back out of her face.

"I think the bed slats either slipped out or broke, and then the mattress fell through."

Candy gazed wide-eyed at the tangle in front of them. "Really? What do you think caused that to happen? We weren't being *that* wild, were we?" She found herself blushing at her question.

Michael dropped his arm around her shoulder and gave her a reassuring squeeze. "No. No, we weren't. I think they were just old, that's all." He didn't believe it for a minute. It was the house. It was haunted by the ghosts of families past, just as Candy had suspected. It didn't approve of an unmarried couple making love within its sacrosanct walls.

Michael's pulse gradually slowed as he glared around the room, his hands on his hips. "I suppose I should be grateful that all that happened was we got dumped on the floor," he muttered as he surveyed the wreckage. "But I want you to know," he informed whoever—or whatever—might be listening, "that while things might have looked bad, I was in perfect control. We would have stopped."

The last corner of the bed slipped through the frame and crashed.

"Okay, okay." Michael threw up his hands in resignation. "So it was iffy. Sue me." But it wasn't iffy now. Thoughts of the commitments to marriage and family made through the past hundred years in this house, in this room, probably even in this bedstead, had him cooled off in nothing flat. "Oh, man, what am I doing?" He ran a hand through his hair. "Well, this place can just darn well put up with us for a few more months. Then we'll be gone, and in the long run, we're doing it a favor."

"Michael, what are you muttering about?"

HOUSEMATES

"Hmm? Oh, nothing. Nothing at all." He tapped his bare foot on the cold floor in a gesture of pure exasperation. "Well, at least the bed's level again," he observed. "I vote we just straighten out the sheets and blankets as best we can and climb back in."

Candy looked at the odd sleeping arrangement Michael was suggesting. They'd have to climb inside a bed frame to sleep on a mattress that was on the floor. She shrugged. Weird, but she guessed it was a fitting end to a decidedly strange day. "Okay, fine. Pull everything back on your side but the top sheet. We'll fix that up first."

It took several moments of tugging, pulling and tucking before order was reinstated.

"There," Michael grunted as he did a flip over the side rail and fell on his back on the mattress. "It's practically dawn. I would dearly love to salvage a few hours' sleep."

Candy climbed over the opposite rail and carefully lay down on her side. "Me, too," she declared.

"So, you stay on your side of the bed and I'll try to stay on mine," Michael continued.

"I beg your pardon?"

"I'm serious. This is basically all your fault."

"What?"

"You heard me. You are incredibly alluring." Michael rolled on his side to face her. "I suppose I could cut off my hands to keep from reaching for you, but it seems a bit drastic. I might need them to get this stupid bed back together."

"Michael, you're being ridiculous." Candy's chest swelled as she huffed.

Michael turned his eyes away. "No, I'm being realistic. You ever do your family tree?"

"Why?" she asked suspiciously.

He shrugged. "Just wondering if there are any sirens coming through in your genetic code. I feel like I'm being lured to my doom. I would dearly love to know the cause of the fire this afternoon...."

"What do you mean by that?"

"What do you want to bet it comes back with a report of undeterminable origins?"

"Michael, is there a point you're trying to make?"

He crossed his arms over his chest as he lay on his back staring up at the ceiling. "We're being pushed together. Can't you see it? The former families are angry at our trespassing. They want us married, just like they were when they lived here, I know it. Look how we're being shoved into close proximity, then not allowed any closer. Take tonight. We're in the same bed for a couple of hours and nothing—everything's hunky-dory. But the first whiff of any impropriety and, bam, we get dumped on the floor." He again ran a hand through his hair. "And listening to the words coming out of my mouth, I think it's safe to assume my mind must have slipped a gear when we got dropped. It's the only logical explanation for this insanity." He rolled on his side and propped a hand under his head. He stared down at her accusingly.

"I'll tell you something else," he offered. "God made a mistake with your genetic code."

"What?"

He nodded, sure of his logic. "Just listen. Here's how I see it going down. Your genetic deck got a bad deal." He waved her silent as her mouth opened in an indignant *O*. "Think about it from my perspective. Here you are, gifted with a body to kill for. Do you know I've never even seen you work out? You just naturally look that way, don't you?"

HOUSEMATES

Candy rolled her eyes and nodded. "But it's not all that great of a body, Michael. I think I found some cellulite on my hips the other day, and if I could lose a little on the top, I might try running, but it's too uncomfortable right now."

"Say any of that in front of my sister and she'll hit you. Anyway, as I was saying, this terrific body is paired with a feminine nesting mind-set that's mind-boggling. You're marriage material," he accused, "and most of the male population in the world could hurt you without even realizing it because they wouldn't be able to see past your chest."

Candy crossed her arms over her breasts and glared at him. "Once more, is there a point to any of this?"

He nodded vigorously. "Yes, there is. We're being set up. I can see it even if you can't. The ghosts in this dump want a family living here. They figure they've got a couple of patsies in us. Force us into the same bed, how can we resist? An unbelievably hot-looking woman, a normal redblooded male. How long can we last just looking without touching? The bed crashed right then to let us know they've got our number, but I won't be pushed into anything, you hear?" Michael asked the question loudly while glancing around the room. Then he turned back to Candy. "So, you just stay over there and leave me alone."

Her anger flared. "Oh, I see. All the responsibility falls on me. How typically male. I suppose it's supposed to be easy for me to ignore shoulders three feet wide and a chest that ripples with muscle?"

He looked at her in amazement. His shoulders turned her on? She liked his chest? "Candy," he explained patiently, "there's nothing special about my physique. You're the one with the body a man would happily sell his soul to the devil to possess."

136 HOUSEMATES

Candy flopped onto her back. "Oh, yeah, right." She turned her head to give him a pitying look. How could he be unaware of his own appeal? He wasn't. He couldn't be. He was full of baloney. Did he think she'd lived her life in a convent? "Listen, Michael, I've been to plenty of pools and beaches, seen plenty of guys in pretty brief stuff, so you can just can the I'm-nothing-special garbage. Evidently this is a mutual problem, one we'll have to work on together. You're not dumping the whole thing on me."

Candy's words replayed themselves in his brain. She'd seen plenty of guys in pretty brief stuff? On the beach? At swimming pools? He must have misheard. Come on, while nobody with any brains played around these days, surely there must have been one or two relationships where she'd really cared enough to, hadn't there? He probed cautiously. "Are you by any remote possibility saying you've never, that is, uh..."

She looked at him curiously. "What?"

"Candy, you're not a virgin, are you?"

She recoiled slightly. "Well, I mean— What business is it of yours?"

He collapsed, one fist over his eyes. "Oh, my God, you are. No wonder they literally yanked the bed right out from under us." He pulled his hand away from his face and glared at her. "You could give a man some warning, you know."

"Warning! You want a warning! I should have a flashing red light on my forehead? Ringing bells? A sign that says Caution, Virgin Crossing?" She turned her back to him and pulled the covers up over her shoulder. "You had it right earlier, you know. Your brain *has* slipped a gear." She plumped the pillow beneath her head rather viciously, then informed him in no uncertain terms, "I'm going back

HOUSEMATES 137

o sleep now. Please don't bother me any further. Good ight."

"I'm moving out," Michael announced baldly once norning had the good grace to arrive. He held up his hand vhen Candy would have argued. "It's the only logical hing to do."

"No, it's not," Candy said immediately. Oh, God, she idn't want to be here by herself, not without Michael. Never mind all those years she'd spent in her own apartnent. This was different. "The real problem here is that ou were being your usual cheap self. Why don't we clean p another bedroom and buy a second mattress-and-spring et?"

Darn his hide. Didn't he feel any of the things she'd ecognized in herself last night? Was she truly alone in this nsanity? "Michael, you said last night you wouldn't be ushed, but do you ever see yourself getting married?" she sked carefully.

"No," he answered baldly, then added, "Don't get me rong. I've often thought about having a woman who oved only me, a son to play ball with. And you were right ne other afternoon when you showed me that butterfly ink-and-blue wallpaper. It'd be great in the small bedoom upstairs for a nursery. But my family is a marital isaster area. I can't take the chance. No son of mine will o through what I did when I came home from camp and ound my father gone."

How the devil did you combat a man determined to stay way from you out of pure altruism? She had no clue. Vasn't life a bite in the buns sometimes? In love for the rst time, and it had to be with a guy who was going to elflessly walk away from her. If she ranted and raved the ay she wanted to, she'd only sound like a shrew, so she

138 HOUSEMATES

stayed seated at the card table where she'd been eating
bowl of cereal and adjusted her suit skirt sharply dow
over her knees. Fortunately it was firmly anchored at he
waist, otherwise she'd have whipped it right off in her ar
gry frustration.

She rubbed the area between her brows. Her head wa
starting to pound. "You know what? I'm not going in
work today. In fact, I'm not going in for the rest of th
week. You do what you like, but since I have to live her
now—by myself—I'm going to spend some time makin
it habitable."

Michael looked around him and sighed. She was righ
A man couldn't expect a woman like Candy to live lik
this. "I'll take the rest of the week off, too," he decided o
the spot. He didn't mind creating an oasis of civility in th
mess for her. She deserved it. She was a trooper, a goo
woman a normal man not carrying all his emotional bag
gage around would snap up in a minute. Provided Cand
let him, of course. There was no doubt in his mind Cand
could hold off a legion of marriage-minded men if she s
chose, which made last night all the less understandabl
"Yes, that's what we'll do," he said. "No one will expe
us to come in, anyway. We've got insurance forms to fi
out and all kinds of other things. Just let me go check i
someplace cheap, maybe the Y, then I'll be back."

Candy blinked. "You know," she began, "there've bee
times this past week when I've begun to suspect that a fe
of your brain's workstations might need replacing. This
ridiculous."

Michael was silent for a minute. She might be righ
Maybe his personal assembly line did need updating. H
certainly seemed to be a glutton for punishment latel
Look at him. Now he was on his way to check into a ho

HOUSEMATES

139

el. "But I won't be pushed," he muttered to himself on his way out the door.

Candy spent the remainder of the week watching Michael circle warily around her. The man literally never came within three feet of her, regardless of the lengths he had to go to maintain that distance.

"He's *angry* that he wants me," she said as she ruthlessly punched her pillow into submission the night before he was due to go back to work. "I mean, I've had guys angry because I wouldn't give them what they wanted, but this is the first time I've ever had anybody angry that I would. Well, he'll pickle himself in paint remover before he gets a second opportunity."

She flopped onto the pillow, trapping it between her stomach and the mattress. "Imagine. Me, a nester! He's crazy. Nuts. The man actually thinks the bed broke because the house didn't approve of what was going on. He's el flippo." And she was disappointed, no matter how she tried to convince herself otherwise.

Candy slept, but not well. Her dreams were full of herself done up head to toe in bright yellow plumage, desperately trying to build a nest in the middle of the old house's master bedroom while Michael, a showy red cardinal, desperately tried to pull it all apart—without touching her. She was exhausted when she dragged herself into work.

"Wow. I figured you were having a rough time of it," Tina said as Candy plunked herself down on her chair with no attempt at finesse whatsoever. "I've never known you to take off any time before. But you look even worse than expected." Her friend hesitated. "Unfortunately I've got news that'll make the past week more complete."

"Oh, crumb. It's Monday. I'm supposed to be making a new start, getting a fresh beginning. Maybe I ought to

140   HOUSEMATES

just go back home and pull the blankets over my head. Try
again tomorrow morning.''

Tina nodded sympathetically. ''Not a bad idea actu
ally.''

''Okay.'' Candy sighed. ''Lay it on me. What now?''

Trying to act nonchalant and failing miserably, Tina
asked, ''Have you by any chance been following the new
the last couple of weeks?''

''Why? Who'd we invade now?'' Candy said suspi
ciously.

''No, it's nothing like that,'' Tina hastily assured her
''It's just that, well, the real-estate market isn't doing very
well right now.''

''It's fall,'' Candy told her friend. ''The market neve
does well in the fall and gets worse in the winter. It'll pick
up in early spring when we're ready to sell,'' she confi
dently predicted.

''Uh, Candy, with a little luck you're right, but I
wouldn't hold your breath if I was you. The papers are
talking about what looks like the start of a major crash
not a seasonal slump. They're saying the bottom is falling
out of the market, if the past few weeks are any indica
tion.''

Candy stared at her, stunned. ''No. I don't believe it.''
Silence reigned for a moment. ''Then again, maybe I do.
often warn people not to get in line behind me at the store
It's inevitable that someone right in front of me will wan
to pay for their whole order with coupons that are usuall
for things they didn't buy. Or the clerk has to turn i
money, or her cash-register tape needs replacing, or it'
time for her break and there's a switching of the guard
or—''

''I get the idea.''

HOUSEMATES   141

"It's just not fair." Candy sniffed. "Mary mentioned it in passing the last time I talked to her, but I didn't pay much attention. Darn it, everybody else makes a fortune doing this kind of thing. How come I'm the one who's going to lose my shirt?"

"Try real hard to hang on to it for a little bit longer," Tina advised, dropping the next bomb. "At least until you've seen Gary Felding. He called several times while you were out last week."

Candy crossed her arms defensively over her breasts. 'Did you explain why I was out?" she asked.

"He didn't seem to care. He just wants to see the contract you're supposed to be preparing."

"What a sweetheart."

"You could sneak out and see him while Michael's preoccupied with his phone call."

Candy swiveled around in her chair and looked over to Michael's desk. He *was* there and looking none too happy with his caller. "When did he come in?" she hissed at Tina. "I never saw him." She'd become so attuned to Michael lately, it seemed as if she ought to have sensed his presence, even if she'd been too distracted to actually notice him come in. Man, she was really weirding out. It was all Michael's fault, of course. She sniffed again. "Well, it doesn't matter. Just because he's here doesn't mean I have to sneak out to Rust-safe. I am a grown woman making a business call. He can just cope."

"I don't know," Tina said. "Might be safer to sneak. Lately I've gotten the impression that there's more to that particular book than just its cover."

"You're not kidding." Candy studied his slumped form. He looked tired and crumpled. She suspected he wasn't feeling any too well, either, judging from the way he had his eyes closed and was massaging his forehead with his

142 HOUSEMATES

hand as he listened. She tried to harden her heart, but found herself asking, "What do you think's wrong with him?"

"Probably the same thing that's wrong with you."

Sexual frustration? Candy sighed and massaged her own forehead. No. That would be easy to write off. Unfortunately her feelings went a lot deeper than that. Too bad Michael's didn't.

Exerting tremendous effort, Candy began reacquainting herself with the papers in her briefcase, honing in on the numbers for Rust-safe. When she felt comfortable once again with the figures, she reached for the phone and hoped Gary Felding hadn't changed his mind.

A hand came around from somewhere behind her and stayed her arm. Candy glanced down in surprise, her heart racing. She'd recognize that hand anywhere. "Michael, you scared the life out of me. What do you want?" As if she didn't know. After the call they'd made together on sleazy Gary, he'd made it quite clear she wasn't to go back there by herself. How had he figured out what she was up to? It was enough to make her believe the man could read minds.

"Candy, I need to talk to you for a few minutes."

She immediately began justifying herself. "I was just going to set up an appointment with him, that's all. I would have—"

"Could we go down to the lounge for a moment?"

He'd taken her elbow and was urging her up out of the chair. She finally got a good look at his face. She must have really been in her own world the past few days not to notice how exhausted he appeared and the way his suit hung off his shoulders even more unwillingly than usual. "My gosh, Michael, have you gotten any sleep at all?"

HOUSEMATES

"Not much," he responded grimly, "and it looks like I'll be getting even less."

"Why?" Candy asked, her concern evident. She wasn't even fighting him as he led her off down the hall. "What's wrong?"

"I'm moving back to the house," he announced baldly.

Candy felt a thrill. He was moving back? He couldn't stay away from her. How exciting. How come he looked so glum? Not exactly a flattering reaction. She felt a frisson of irritation and said ironically, "That's too bad, Michael. I'm sorry to hear that."

Michael stopped in his tracks and stared at her. "You are? Really?"

"You acted like you were announcing a death in the family," she told him impatiently. "What kind of reaction was I supposed to have?"

They'd reached the lounge. Michael kicked the door shut with his foot the moment he had her over the threshold.

"You just slammed the door in Steve's face," she said.

"He's lucky I didn't slam it *on* his face. You think I don't see the way he's always checking you out? Stupid blond-god types. You're old enough to see through that fake tanned facade by now."

She faced him. "Do you see me dating him? Do you? And besides, what business is it of yours? You've made no bones about the fact that you're not interested."

Michael stared down at her, making an obvious attempt to hang on to his temper. Silent numbers formed on his lips. She wished, just once, he'd let it go—that they could have a real wingding of an argument. She had a few pithy remarks she wouldn't mind letting fly. But Michael had been scarred by parents who argued, and not for the

144 HOUSEMATES

world would she hurt him further. That was a part of love, she guessed. Biting your tongue if that's what it took.

Michael sighed and looked away. "This isn't getting us anywhere." He pulled a chair out from the long table running down the center of the employee lounge. "Here, sit down." He took a chair right around the corner of the table from Candy's. Rubbing his eyes tiredly, he confessed, "I've just had some bad news, so I'm not in the best possible mood at the moment. Sorry for jumping on you."

The man certainly had a knack for making her feel guilty. "What's happened now? How could our run of bad luck get any worse?"

"Well, it just did," he admitted as he sprawled back in his chair. "Man, it's ten o'clock in the morning, and I'm exhausted. This is unbelievable. I'm twenty-six and I feel like an old, old man."

"Tell me what happened. Was it that phone call?" Candy covered his hand with one of her own. It was warm, strong and totally incongruous with the beaten form in front of her. Sympathetically, she twined her fingers with his.

He looked at her with bleak eyes. "That was my sister on the phone. She and her husband are splitting up."

Chapter Nine

"Your sister's getting divorced," Candy repeated carefully. His family must be very close-knit for him to feel his sister's divorce so keenly. "That's really a shame. Marriage breakups are always traumatic. Are you and your sister close?"

Michael continued to study their entwined fingers. In fact, he lifted their hands off the table, holding them up as if for a closer look. The expression on his face became almost wistful. "You don't get it, do you?"

Candy looked from their hands to his face. "No, I don't think I do. Do you want to explain it to me?"

He sighed. It was long and heartfelt. "It affects me— us—in a couple of different ways."

"I'm sorry, Michael, but I don't see how."

He looked her straight in the eye. "It's the final failure."

Candy digested that. The final failure. It sounded so...final.

Michael continued, "It means, as of right now, there is not a single successful first marriage in the whole family. My sister, my parents, neither of whom has had a successful *second* marriage, thank you, my grandparents, *their* parents. God only knows how far back it goes."

"We talked about this briefly before. You're convinced that any marriage you contracted would fail, right? Because of the history of bad marriages in your family?"

Michael's eyes had still not lifted from the small hand entangled with his own much larger one. "Candy, we're both mechanical engineers, trained in the sciences and logical thinking. Think about it. Statistically, my chances are just about zilch for happily-ever-after."

He sat quietly for a moment, thinking. "I wish I could put my finger on the reason my parents couldn't make it work." He shook his head. "But to the best of my knowledge, there wasn't one. They just couldn't. Neither one cheated on the other, drank or was physically abusive. There was no gambling away the paycheck at the track, no high-stress job, yet there was always enough money for the basics. Don't you see? If I could just say, aha, here's what the problem was, then I could take a chance. I'd know what to avoid. But I haven't learned anything, not from any of their failures, because I can't figure out what lesson was being taught."

Michael's pain was obvious, but Candy didn't know how to soothe it. She was hurting herself. She'd been willing to give herself to him the other night because she'd thought they might have a future together. But Michael wasn't just holding off on making a commitment, he'd written it off for all time. She felt his pain right then, but she also suffered her own. My gosh, she'd just spent the past week if not in hell, then certainly purgatory as she'd watched Michael distance himself from her.

HOUSEMATES

147

"I don't think you give yourself enough credit," Candy stated carefully. She knew without a doubt she was fighting for her future happiness. "Look how you've bent over backward to always fight fair, to always try to reach a workable compromise." Well, almost always.

Michael continued as if he hadn't heard her. "The studies are there—they've all been done. A child is almost certain to fashion a marriage after his or her parents'. The annoying thing is it's all done on a subconscious level. How do you fight your subconscious?" He placed an absent kiss in her palm, then released it. "I thought I was content. I thought I'd accepted it."

"And then along came this house and me."

Michael nodded. "Exactly. You turned me on like no one I've ever seen before. I thought if I could just have you for a brief time, it would be enough."

She didn't like that, but she could understand it.

"But that house is just such a *family* kind of place." He paused.

"It is, isn't it?"

"Yeah, and I don't know, watching you flit around fixing it up as though we'd be living there, instead of just painting it white for a quick cold resale, well, it got me thinking again."

He looked so tortured Candy found it painful to maintain eye contact. She didn't feel all that hot herself. She'd made an intellectual decision to delay marriage. That was different from being scarred. She had to wonder if it was even possible for Michael to respond to love at this point in his life.

"I can't do it," he burst out, making her jump as he slapped the tabletop. "I won't be responsible for raising another crop of scarred children."

148   HOUSEMATES

And there it was in a nutshell. She could feel his yearning, but doubted he'd ever reach out and take what he wanted. God, she was depressed.

Maybe somebody—something—*had* been looking out for her best interests when the bed had broken. "Michael," she asked, "do you still believe the bed dropped out from under us last Friday night to keep us from, well, you know?"

"I don't know." He leaned back, away from the table, and stretched his arms out in front of him. His fingers were meshed tightly together, palms out as he sought to ease his fatigue. "In my saner moments, of course not. The problem is there haven't been too many of those lately."

And that was a fact.

"I just can't get away from this feeling of being trapped in some intricate web that's bigger than the both of us. For the life of me, though, I can't figure it out. Sometimes I can almost feel my puppet strings being jerked. And I'll tell you something else. Whatever force it is out there that's operating on us is extremely creative. Some of the opportunities being used to throw us together are not to be believed. Put a professional matchmaker to shame, that's for sure."

He drew his fingertips to his chest in a gesture of self-indictment. "I admit we started the whole thing by deciding to go in together on the house, and maybe the house didn't appreciate being viewed as nothing but a money cow—a means rather than an end—but this is no longer funny."

She had to admit it had been a while since she'd enjoyed a good laugh.

Michael threw up his hands in a dramatic gesture. "I mean, come on! We're both burned out of our apartments. It looks like the real-estate market is crashing big

HOUSEMATES 149

time—we'll never sell the place if it does. I try to do the right thing after literally being thrown out of your bed, and now look—I've got to move back! My sister has two little kids under five. She's going to need whatever money I can send her until the paperwork goes through and her husband's forced to fork over some support.''

Michael heaved himself out of his chair and began to roam the room restlessly.

Candy watched, her eyes following his every move.

Suddenly he swung around and faced her. ''I'm getting scared,'' he said as he raked his hand through his hair. ''Which is not a very macho thing to admit, but there you have it.''

''Don't be ridiculous. You're too secure in your masculinity to worry about appearing macho,'' she said in a tone that brooked no argument. And it was true. Michael was deeply male in a way that defied categorizing. God knew she'd been trying for the past several months without much success. It was just there, and everything feminine in her responded to it like, well, like when her mother knocked over the box of straight pins she used for sewing and used a magnet to draw them all back up in one fell swoop. Like that.

''It's your unwillingness to let the past stay in the past that's got me concerned,'' she went on. ''Two months ago, I'd have laughed at this, but here's what I think. The house isn't upset because we were going to break the chain of committed couples living there. No, it simply figured out long before either one of us that we're right for it and in its own way is trying to tell us it doesn't want us passing it on in a couple of months.''

He half rose out of his chair. ''That's silly.''

''Not as silly as some of the explanations you've come up with. This'll give you a laugh. Last Friday I'd decided it was right. We were right for each other. That was the real reason I decided to sleep with you. But the ghost of families past saw right through you, didn't it, Mr. I-can't-make-a-commitment-because-some-day-in-the-unforeseeable-future-things-might-go-wrong?''

Both their heads swung around as the lounge door opened a crack and what appeared to be a disembodied head peeked through. They both glared at the intruder. "What do you want?'' they asked together.

They were thinking, acting and talking in concert for once, Candy realized. She smothered a snicker. Obviously a match made in heaven. Michael heard the choked laugh, though, and turned his glare on her. Immediately she folded her hands on the table in front of her and straightened her posture. "Yes, Tina?'' she asked in a far more civilized voice than before. "Did you need to talk to one of us?''

"No," Tina announced from her position of safety behind the door. "Nobody wants to talk to you. It's been obvious all morning you're both in weird moods. Basically we were just wondering if you'd move your tête-à-tête somewhere else. Several of us are hungry and we want to microwave some popcorn.''

Candy flushed red. "I didn't realize we'd been in here that long," she muttered.

"Don't worry about it," Tina advised. "We all know you've had a rough week. But now that you do know it, could we please come in at least long enough to nuke some snacks?''

"Oh, yes. Of course." Candy had never felt quite so flustered. She rose quickly to leave the room, although how she'd face an office full of coworkers who'd never seen her any way but in control, she couldn't quite imagine.

HOUSEMATES 151

Michael grabbed her arm, preventing her from rising completely. "No," he stated firmly, shocking Candy and, from the look on her face, Tina, as well. "We'll be out in a few minutes. When we're done."

Arching her brows at Candy, Tina said, "This is interesting. Who'd have thought it? Quiet, refined Michael, so forceful and protective around you. I may have to stop by this house of yours and see you two in action."

"Tina," Candy hissed, "get out of here. You're purposely trying to cause trouble."

"Who me? Wouldn't dream of it."

"Out!" Michael ordered.

"I'm gone," Tina said, slowly closing the door. "But not for long, so steam it up and kiss and make up."

"We weren't fighting—not exactly," Candy said. "It was more of a discussion."

Tina shrugged. "So reach a consensus and clear out of the lounge. We're all hungry. Oh, and by the way, you might want to lower your voices. They're carrying all the way down the hall." Tina shut the door.

When they were alone again, Candy shot an embarrassed look at Michael. "I feel really stupid now," she said. "God only knows how many of them are out there and what they heard."

"Forget it," Michael ordered. "We've got too much other stuff to work out to worry about anything else."

He was probably right. She was beginning to hate that about him. "Okay," she said. "We can't possibly take any more time off work. I have got to see Gary Felding, and you—"

"No."

She blinked. "No what?"

He leaned forward. She believed he was trying to intimidate her. It was working, too.

152 HOUSEMATES

"No, you are not going to see Gary Felding. At least not by yourself."

"Don't start on that, Michael," she warned. "Now, when we get out of here, we're going to buy another mattress and spring. We'll set up one of the other bedrooms, okay?"

"The object is to save money," he reminded her.

She smiled kindly. "Believe me, I haven't forgotten. Your only other alternative, however, is for you to sleep on the floor, as I am not about to allow you to share a bed with me until you're ready for something slightly more meaningful than an attempt at working me out of your system. *Capisce?*"

He nodded glumly. "You've made yourself abundantly clear. Look but don't touch. We'll both be insane by the end of the first full week. You just remember this was all your idea when we're babbling like idiots in a few days."

With any luck, he'd come to his senses before then and realize what he was letting slide through his fingers, she told herself grimly. If not, she foresaw major outlays for psychiatric care in the near future. He was right. With the sexual pull both of them felt pulsing off the walls and around the limited confines of their new home, it was going to be a darned unnatural situation. "We'll have to see who cracks first," was all she said.

Michael glared at her briefly, then leaned back in his chair and covered his eyes with his hand. "Man, my life is unraveling right before my eyes. Tell me this, oh, keeper of the marital flame, where am I going to get the money to send my sister if I buy another bed set tonight?"

"We'll buy it out of house funds." Candy held up her hand to forestall his automatic complaint. "No, fair's fair. We bought the first one that way, too. We can put a cou-

HOUSEMATES 153

ple of the projects at the house on hold. The kitchen, for example.''

"We're never going to finish things and get the place back on the market at this rate," he moaned.

"Yes, well, no rush, is there? I mean, with the market collapsing, we wouldn't want it to get stale sitting there with a For Sale sign out front, anyway, would we? Then everyone would think there was something wrong with it."

There was. The place was cursed. But rising from his chair, he capitulated. "Okay, fine. I give up. You win. But as you say, fair's fair. Cast about your family. See if you can come up with a destitute relative. May as well help somebody on your side, as well."

Candy rose, too, relieved to have their little discussion drawing to a close without her bursting into tears from the sense of loss she felt. "If I don't get cracking and get something accomplished around here today, I won't have to look far. It'll probably be me out of work and destitute."

"Which reminds me. I want to hear everything Gary Felding had to say after you call him. Understand? You are not to go over there without me."

"Michael," she hissed under her self-conscious smile as they opened the door and faced the lineup of coworkers impatiently waiting with microwave-popcorn bags in hand, "would you please can the Neanderthal routine?"

"Candy," he hissed right back as he nodded to a few friends, "don't bother trying to threaten me. If you think *I'm* Neanderthal, let me tell you I've asked around about your friend Gary. What I heard was not reassuring. The man clearly got left several steps back on the evolutionary path. Darwin would have loved the guy. You must have had your brains knocked out your ears the night the bed collapsed to even *consider* going over there alone." They

154 HOUSEMATES

neared the end of the gauntlet and Michael sighed with relief as he steered her toward her desk. "There. We made it."

She sat, which was a mistake. Michael, who wasn't even quite six foot, now towered over her.

"I've given in on virtually everything else, Candy, but not this. It's too important. I'm going with you."

"What?" Tina prodded as soon as Michael had left. "What has he given in on?"

Candy frowned at Michael's retreating back. "I don't know," she finally said. "I can't think of a single thing. I thought we'd been reaching compromises all this time. God knows we spent enough time arguing our various positions." Thoughtfully she reached for her Rolodex and Gary Felding's number. Basically all the males in her life right then were, for one reason or another, complete enigmas to her. It might be best to simply cut her losses.

"You know what?" she asked Tina as she flipped to the *F*'s. "I've been thinking. I'm not sure I'm going to do any wallpapering at the house, after all."

"Really? Why not?"

"A nice, quick white paint job would make everything look clean and bright for a lot less money, you know."

"I suppose..."

"And I'd feel bad if the new people came in and I found out they ripped all my papering down. After all, their taste might be completely different. They might want, oh, I don't know, yellow or... purple."

"Yuck."

Candy fingered the card with Gary Felding's number on it. "Yes, well, there's no accounting for taste, is there? I mean, look at this." She pointed to the open Rolodex. "Some woman, of her own free will, actually married this slime. Now me, I've changed my mind completely. I'm

HOUSEMATES 155

telling you, I've just declared the whole timetable I've scheduled my life on since I was sixteen null and void.''

Tina's eyes widened from a squint mode—she'd been attempting to read Candy's Rolodex from her own desk—to an expression of sheer amazement. ''You can't do that! You're within months of achieving all your goals.''

Candy shrugged as she began to punch Rust-safe's phone number into her phone with the eraser end of her pencil. ''Yes, well, the idea was to attain certain professional and personal levels early on, before I found somebody I wanted to marry. That way my hypothetical marriage and children would be under less strain. The children could have braces when they needed them, not have to rely on hand-me-downs from cousins, and go away to good colleges if they had the grades. I couldn't possibly be resentful of him or them and they couldn't be of me because we'd be secure— Yes, Mr. Felding, please. Thank you.''

''And now?'' Tina asked cautiously as Candy waited on hold.

''And now I've suddenly had this blinding realization. Who the heck did I think I was going to marry? My gosh, Mom's already got my dad, and the rest of them aren't worth the powder it would take to blow them up. No, the thing to do is give the house a quick face-lift. You know, clean it up and paint it—cosmetic stuff—try our best to sell it, then take my share, buy a little bungalow and adopt cats— Gary? Yes, it's Candy Barr at Nelson Robotics returning your call....''

Laughing quietly, Tina went back to her own paperwork as Candy placated the manager of Rust-safe.

Forty minutes later, she was finally able to hang up on dear old Gary. She'd ignored every innuendo Gary had dropped—and they'd fallen as thick and fast as floppy disks used to crash on the old computer systems. She'd stuck right to business, and that's what she'd continue to do. Sighing with the difficulty of that particular task, she called up one of Nelson Robotics' standard contracts on her screen and entered the changes she'd need to customize it for Robeson's Rust-safe. With a flick of a button, she printed out a couple of copies and went to see if her branch manager was in his office.

"Bob, can I have a couple of minutes of your time?"

"Yeah, sure. Come on in, Candy." The big man she'd called boss for the past three years looked up from his position behind a mammoth but utilitarian wood-look desk and pointed to the seat across from him. "You got problems?"

Candy looked down at the contract in her hands. At this point in time, guys like Gary Felding were the least of her troubles. Dealing with Michael moving back into the house tonight loomed far larger in her mind than a few double entendres from a middle-aged clown with patent-leather hair.

She forced a smile. "Problems? Don't be silly." There was nothing Bob or anybody else could do about the hash she'd made of her life recently, anyway. And Bob had more or less treated her as his protégée. He'd hired her over several equally qualified men. He took personal pleasure in her achievements and used every one of them as proof to the main office that promoting women was good business, not merely quota filling. The last thing she wanted to do right then was disappoint him or arouse his protective instincts. She couldn't deal with another upset male in her life. So she kept that smile pasted on her lips and put the paperwork down on the desk in front of him.

"What I've got right here in my hot little hands," she said, "is a major sale to Rust-safe. All that's required are

HOUSEMATES

your initials by the changes I've made to the boilerplate contract, dear Mr. Felding's signature, and I'll have made club. Miami, here I come."

Bob Nelson's posture straightened as he perked up and reached for the contract. He began perusing the print. "Rust-safe? No kidding. I knew it wasn't a mistake giving you that account. Just a question of outwaiting them. Once they finally got it through their thick heads they'd have to have a better reason for me to assign a new account exec to them than Felding's simply not wanting to deal with a woman, I knew they'd come through. This is wonderful, Candy. Just wonderful. Congratulations."

Candy cleared her throat and made a little disparaging gesture with her hands. She couldn't do it. It wasn't right. "Well, Bob, to tell you the truth, Michael Cane sort of softened Felding up for me. Otherwise, I think Felding would have quite willingly waited for his assembly line to fall down around his ears before buying anything from me. By the time Michael was done with him, Gary couldn't wait to sign on the dotted line."

Bob's surprise showed on his face. "Cane went with you on a call? He never mentioned it to me. It's not his territory. How did that happen?"

"It's a long story," Candy responded dryly. "Suffice it to say Gary saw the sweet light of reason and is now dying to do business with us."

Bob looked intrigued. "Interesting," he said. "What did Cane threaten him with?"

Candy sank into the chair across from her manager and gave him a wry smile. She could see the humor of the whole thing, but only now, in retrospect. "Oh, there were no threats," she assured him. "Michael was about as subtle as one of our huge mainframe computers hulking next to a little portable desktop. But no threats."

158 HOUSEMATES

Bob leaned forward. "So what'd he do?"

Candy shrugged. "He told a little story."

"A story?"

"Yes." She nodded. "A story about a customer he used to have back at his old location who had a reputation of never buying from women reps. Michael pointed out his disbelief that anyone could be so absolutely medieval in this day and age. Then he proceeded to tell of the bad press that was generated when word of this fellow's backward attitude leaked out, and of how the company hierarchy had been so embarrassed they'd fired the guy. Then Michael very sorrowfully pointed out how, last he heard, the guy was still looking for a job, and here it was, over a year later."

"Sounds a bit on the subtle side for our friend Felding. He understood he was being threatened?" Bob chuckled.

"Oh, he got the point real fast." Candy grinned in return. "It was all very embarrassing, but extremely effective. I've made club, thanks to Michael."

Bob gave her a shrewd look. "I'd still like to know how he happened to go along on the call with you in the first place."

"Michael has a way of getting his way when he wants to," she assured him. "He's a darn good salesman. We're lucky to have him here."

"I'm glad to hear you say that, Candy," Bob admitted. "For a while there, you seemed to resent him. You're both top drawer. You'd make a good team, you know that?"

Yes, she knew that. The light had dawned. Too bad Michael was still wandering around in the dark. "Michael's an unusual man. It just took me a while to see it."

"I heard you two bought a house together," Bob offered.

HOUSEMATES 159

"Don't remind me." She shuddered. "We're going to end up killing each other. Whether it'll be by accident or design is all that remains to be seen."

Bob chuckled again. "I just thought of something. You know the old saw about the lady protesting too much? What if you guys end up interested in each other? What if you ended up *married?* You'd be Candy Cane. Ever think of that?"

"Constantly. All the time. But I discovered recently all my worries were for nothing. There's no chance. Now give me back that contract and leave me alone. I've got stuff to do."

Bob's laughter chased her down the hall.

When Candy finished for the day, she went to a fast-food drive-through, then headed for the house. They were having a thirty-five-cent-burger special, so let Michael try to complain. Her temper had been rising all day and she'd enjoy shoving one down his throat right about then. Imagine his deciding a marriage between them would end in divorce before they'd even *agreed* to take any vows, let alone speak them. Talk about a negative attitude. *She'd* actually considered being Candy Cane for the rest of her life. That would certainly teach her to be self-sacrificing in the name of true love. True love, ha! Michael wouldn't know true love if it came up and bit him on the butt. Let him go buy his own dumb bed. She had better things to do.

She parked on the two narrow concrete ribbons of her driveway and slid out of the car. Once inside the house, she tightened the bulbs in the wall sconces until they threw a delicate light into the living room. Finding a spot on the wall where the Spanish-style stucco finish wasn't too rough, she sank to the floor, supporting her back with the wall. Absently glancing around, she enjoyed the fragile

160 HOUSEMATES

yellow light the electric candles cast about the room. You know, it really could be a lovely house. The living room practically screamed with potential. Her hand itched to take up a paintbrush right then, exhausted as she was.

Unwrapping a hamburger and taking a bite, she wondered how difficult it would be to put a switch on the lights so they didn't have to be controlled by screwing and unscrewing the bulbs. Certainly she had no idea how to do it. Her eyes narrowed and she chewed more vigorously. Michael would want to read a book on the subject and attempt the task himself. End up getting electrocuted—not that that was such a bad idea.

"Damn," she muttered and was startled by the sound of her voice echoing in the empty room. It wasn't like her to be vindictive. She couldn't believe the direction her thoughts were taking. But still, she felt like the proverbial woman scorned, which was ridiculous. Michael wasn't scorning her. To his convoluted way of thinking, he was trying to protect her from him, which was *really* ridiculous.

She swallowed and leaned her head back against the wall, momentarily closing her eyes. How had she gotten herself into this mess?

Window shopping with Michael while waiting for possession of this architectural gem and now working on the place together had captured every bit of her free time. Her social life had ended with the entering of their bid last August. One had to wonder if Michael had planned it that way. Shame immediately colored her cheeks at such a thought.

However, the fact remained that she was now in a position where her every waking moment was filled with thoughts of a guy whose last name was a personal nightmare come to life. She should be wildly grateful to Mi-

HOUSEMATES

chael for stopping things the other night. She should be down on her knees kissing the ground he walked on for keeping her from taking on a handicap that would haunt her the rest of her business career. Who would take an executive named Candy Cane seriously? Nobody, that's who.

Unfortunately she didn't feel grateful. She was angry. And hurt. Well, she'd have to get over that if they were going to be living together the next few months. Darn his sister, anyway. Darn his parents, his grandparents and his whole stupid divorce-ridden family, too. How come their respective houses had never dropped *their* beds out from under *them* when things had started getting hot and heavy? Some houses had no sense of pride. They'd let anybody in the front door.

Oh, God, she was getting as crazy as Michael.

Candy took several deep breaths and tired to capture a bit of something resembling serenity. She focused on her surroundings, instead of on the upsetting images of Michael and his relationship-retarded family.

The house in which she sat was turn-of-the-century, as far as the realtors had been able to figure out. Thoughts of previous families teased her. Two, maybe three generations had grown to maturity within these walls. Had they been happy? Had any one of the fathers hung a swing from the sturdy limbs of the old maple out back so their children could play in its shade, safe in the fenced confines of the yard? Had those kids grown up untarnished by life's cruelties? Had the parents grown old gracefully, dying peacefully here at home in their own beds? Who had painted the outside trim forest-green? And who the Wedgwood blue that peeked through where the green had flaked off?

Candy had no idea how long her mind drifted, but she napped back to reality when a car door slammed just

162 HOUSEMATES

outside the French doors. It didn't take a genius to figure out who had arrived. She scrubbed her eyes with the back of her hand to remove any trace of melancholia-induced moisture. She also decided then and there to have the wall sconces taken care of without Michael's knowledge. He may be a jerk, but he didn't deserve to die. He was, she acknowledged with a sigh, well-intentioned.

The front doorknob protested, the door's hinges actually squealed, and then Michael was there, walking briskly into the living room where the only light shone. He stopped when he saw her. "Hi."

"Hi, yourself," Candy returned, her eyes a bit watery. She was still lost in the two or three generations of children who'd used the house in its prime. Had they played hopscotch out on the front terrace?

Oh, damn, she silently wailed. Michael was doing it to her again. Where had he found a place to change his clothes? She was going to have to figure out some way to convince him to work on the house while wearing one of his business suits. It was too late for tonight. He was already in jeans and a soft flannel shirt that did nothing to hide the breadth of his shoulders. How was she supposed to get over him if he insisted in parading around like that? She could feel herself warm up as her heart began pumping blood through her system with a lot more force than necessary. Michael in jeans did that to her. What a sad fact of life.

Chapter Ten

Cautiously Michael squatted in front of her. "How come you haven't changed out of your work clothes?" he asked as he studied her face.

She simply shrugged. She hadn't because she hadn't. Period.

"You'll ruin your good clothes sitting in all this dust, and you haven't got all that many of them left," he continued. Then with hand extended, he coaxed, "Come on. I'll give you a boost up so you can go put on some grubbies. I thought we'd pull down the dining-room ceiling tonight so it doesn't collapse on us some time when we're not looking. But maybe you're getting sick?"

Candy smiled limply at Michael's concern. "I'm fine, Michael. Really. I was just thinking about something you said. You're right, you know. This place is a memory trap. Sort of a generic *Christmas Carol*, complete with the ghost of children past. When you're in here, you can't help but think about all those long-gone families. This would have

164 HOUSEMATES

been perfect for them. It's big enough for children, but not so large the parents would have had to move when the kids were grown.''

Michael glanced around. ''Yeah, in its prime, this house would have been terrific, I've got to admit. But are you sure you're okay? I was going to bring in the twin mattress set I bought and then work in the dining room like I said, but I can stay here with you if you'd like.'' He snapped his fingers. ''I could call somebody for you. How about your mother?''

Candy snorted. Her mother, the originator of ''Don't make the same mistake I made and fall in love too early,'' was still convinced that falling in love could be managed and put on a schedule. She'd be horrified by Candy's current condition. ''Michael?''

''Yeah, honey?''

Oh, God. She grew warmer as her heart pumped harder, evidently unable to handle an endearment from Michael. ''You know what?''

''No, what?''

''Let's not pull down the dining-room ceiling tonight. Know what I want to do, instead?''

''Sit in the corner and suck your thumb while you feel overwhelmed by the enormity of the task we've got here?''

''No. I'm not even that ambitious. I want to just sit here. Waste the whole night. Maybe build a fire in the fireplace. What do you think?''

Michael's eyes widened and his head recoiled slightly. This was asking for trouble. He hadn't even gotten his own mattress and box spring into the house after his week away and she already wanted to play with fire. She probably meant it literally, while it was the figurative interpretation that was doing him in.

He eased his body down next to hers and took a cautious bite of the hamburger dangling from her fingertips.

His brain needed a certain amount of fortification to think this one through.

"I noticed a small woodpile next to the garage the other day. I guess I could build a fire," he offered reluctantly. This was stupid, really stupid. As far as he was concerned, the function of a fire in a fireplace had narrowed to only one purpose after central heating became the accepted standard, and that was the furthering of romance. Candy, on the other hand, was all caught up in some kind of nostalgia. She didn't know what she was asking for.

The house would not be pleased with them. He just knew it. One could only imagine the retribution it might come up with.

"Think of all the people who've sat in front of a fire in this very room," she said.

Michael stifled a groan as he wondered how many of them had gone from sitting to lying to starting their families on a rug in front of it.

"There's a stack of newspapers on the back porch," Candy remembered. "And matches in the kitchen. I'll get them if you get some logs."

Michael stood and left the room, resigned to his fate.

When he returned laden with logs, Candy was kneeling in front of the fireplace crumpling newspaper into tight balls. Wads of them covered the hearth. Michael knelt next to her, letting the logs tumble free of his arms. God, she smelled good. A certain sense of inevitability crept over him as he breathed deeply of her womanly fragrance—so quintessentially feminine and yet at the same time so uniquely hers. There was no denying that the forces at play here were larger than the two of them. But hey, what kind of hand was left for fate to play? They were already on the floor, after all. He was going to kiss her.

Gently, so as not to spook her in her odd mood, he let his hands settle on her shoulders and turned her to face him. First, he tried a nonthreatening forehead kind of kiss, then moved on to the tip of her nose. Only then did he claim her mouth.

Oh, man, he'd known this was going to be a mistake. There was no such thing as a little light lovemaking with Candy Barr. The woman had incendiary lips. Who needed newspapers and matches with her around, he wondered as heat spread with annoying rapidity through his body. Candy's lips could ignite the logs without any help. All he had to do was aim her puckered mouth in the general direction of the fireplace. Damn, she was lethal.

Well, whatever larger-than-life forces were out there waiting to see if he was going to behave himself could just hold their pants on until he got the fire lit, which was never going to happen if he didn't somehow manage to pry his lips loose and arrange the wood on the hearth. Still, he couldn't stop himself from running his tongue around the corners of her mouth before reluctantly breaking contact. Leaning his forehead against hers, he tried to regulate his breathing. This evening was going to be torture. If only Candy was more herself. No, even then she really was the marrying kind and he . . . well, he just wasn't.

You know what? Whoever or whatever kept pushing them together could just deal with what it'd started, he decided, suddenly feeling rebellious. He was going to do it, right down to bringing in the wine, cheese and crackers he'd bought and never used the first night he and Candy had spent together in the house. They would take whatever time they had together and use it to the fullest. He'd make sure she had no regrets when it ended—and he knew it must end.

Determinedly he made a torch out of rolled newspaper and held it up the chimney to heat the flue. "And you can just stay out of this," he growled, glaring at all four corners of the room.

HOUSEMATES

"You say something?"

"No, nothing. Just talking to myself."

"Oh."

Yes, oh. Michael lit the paper crumbled under the logs next, narrowing his eyes as he did so. Oh, yes. Tonight was the night.

They'd both been on their knees, working on setting the fire. Then, simultaneously, they turned to face each other, still on their knees. Michael lifted both hands, palms up, and Candy matched hers to them, palm to palm.

She wasn't going to fight him, he thought exultantly. *She wanted him as much as he wanted her. Everything would be fine.*

He inhaled deeply and immediately began to choke. "What the devil?"

Smoke was billowing into the room. He looked in astonishment from Candy to the fire merrily pumping smoke at them, then back to Candy. His eyes were already smarting and he noticed hers were tearing, as well.

He swore fervently. "I can't figure out what could be wrong," he said as he rubbed irritated eyes. All thoughts of romance were dead. "I opened the flue. I know I did."

"Well, something's wrong," Candy gasped. "This is awful. Open the windows and doors, quick."

They'd built a good fire. It had blazed up quickly, and now they had difficulty putting it out. Michael had to balance burning logs on the end of the shovel they'd used to clear the room of trash. He tossed them out onto the patio outside the French doors, then revised his estimate on the number of children whose journey in life had started in front of this particular hearth.

The infusion of outside air gradually cleared the room. Michael attempted to look up the chimney, hoping against hope to find some physical reason for the evening's failure. "There's got to be some kind of problem here," he

168　　　　　　　　　　　HOUSEMATES

declared judiciously with absolutely no clue what he was looking for. "We'll have to have an expert come in."

"I'll call one tomorrow," Candy vowed as she shivered by the open French doors. "For now, though, I give up. I'll help you with your bed set, then I'm calling it a night."

Michael looked down at her, then at the logs still smoking out on the patio. There was no doubt in his mind this was another heavy-handed example of the house's mean-spirited intervention. It was out to get him. *Thanks a lot, buddy.* He touched two fingers to his forehead in silent salute. *Thanks a whole lot.*

Disappointed, he agreed to terminate the evening.

A long overdue cold front—it was early November, after all, and he could hardly complain although he desperately wanted to—came through that night, and Michael shivered in his solitary twin bed. Warming the sheets was definitely a job for two, and if he was chilled, petite Candy must be frozen through. The noble thing to do would be to slip into the master bedroom and offer his slightly warmer body to Candy's undoubtedly icy one. That said, he hated to think what kind of unpleasantness the ever resourceful ghost of families past would conjure up should he attempt such a feat.

Finally, just after midnight, he gave up. Noises from down the hall told him Candy was still awake, probably too cold to sleep. He was going to have to get up and tackle the boiler, that was all there was to it.

He stalked past Candy's open doorway to the bathroom. When he was finished there, he peeked into her bedroom as he went by. Immediately she sat up.

"Are you okay, Michael?"

"Other than all my extremities turning blue from the cold, I'm fine."

Candy pulled her blanket and spread more tightly around her. "It's really chilly in here tonight, isn't it? I'm

HOUSEMATES

not sure we're going to make it the next two weeks until the new boiler gets installed without freezing to death.''

"We're not even going to try," he informed her. "I'm going down to the basement right now and try a little arm wrestling with that many-armed bandit masquerading as a heating agent down there."

She sat up straighter. "You're going to get the old boiler to work?''

Michael thought of the ancient relic lurking two stories down. The old behemoth took up a good half of the basement. It hadn't reached its current age without being stubborn. He was sure he'd have his hands full. "I'm not making any guarantees," he warned. "But it's worked seventy years or more already. With any luck, we ought to be able to coax another two weeks out of it."

"Michael, you get some heat going in this place and I'll be your slave forever," Candy promised fervently.

For all the good it would do him, Michael thought to himself. He hadn't managed to get anywhere with her yet. He doubted the house would be impressed enough by even willing slavery to let him start now.

Candy pushed the blankets down and swung her feet over the side of the bed. "In fact," she announced, "I'm so cold I'm willing to go down into that dark creepy basement with you and help."

Michael did not want Candy to witness what he was sure would degenerate into a debacle. His abilities would be taxed enough without having to juggle what came out of his mouth along with everything else. "No, no. Stay up here under the blankets. No sense in both of us freezing down there. I'll figure it out. Just give me a few minutes."

"My money's on you," she assured him. "But don't you want me to at least come hold the flashlight or something? That overhead bulb down there doesn't throw much light, I've noticed."

170 HOUSEMATES

"No! I mean, that's all right, don't worry about it. I can handle it. Just listen for any loud crashes."

"Well, okay..."

He left before she could change her mind. She'd already been shivering violently from just those few moments out from under the blankets. He'd have to figure this thing out quickly, and he would figure it out, by God. There was more than his innate stubbornness at play here, he realized as he went down the steps to the low-ceilinged dark basement girded with nothing but a flashlight and a book of matches as protection against the peppering of small-scale wildlife that hung out in such places. Yes, it was more than stubbornness. There was also his determination to make Candy more comfortable.

With that thought troubling him, he forgot to duck his head and banged it where the ceiling came in low over the stairs. By the time he was kneeling in front of the boiler, grimly rubbing grime off the small print he found on one side, he was already swearing.

Candy joined him forty-five minutes later. Michael brought his off-color suggestions of what the boiler could do with itself down to a low mutter. He also changed his position from a kneel to a sit. Kneeling might give Candy the impression he'd been pleading with the thing—or praying to it. Neither option was likely to impress her.

"Michael?"

He acted surprised. "Oh, you're down here. Something wrong?"

After a careful visual check, she sat gingerly on the bottom step and huddled more deeply into her full-length velour robe. "I was just wondering how things were going."

"Fine. Everything's going just fine."

She cocked her head. His tone of voice was a dead giveaway. "It's awfully late. Maybe we should just call it

HOUSEMATES

171

night. We could call a heating contractor in the morning," she offered hopefully.

Michael wondered if his wallet was upstairs in that godforsaken bedroom sprouting wings and a halo. The way it was hemorrhaging lately, it surely wouldn't last long in this world. "No way," he exclaimed. "We'll be paying that guy enough in a couple of weeks."

"It was just an idea," Candy said and shivered.

"Well, forget it. I've almost got this thing licked, anyway. I just need a few more minutes."

Candy perked up. "Really? Here, I'll hold the flashlight. It's hard to see back in the corners."

He didn't want to see back in the corners. God alone knew what might be exposed with a little illumination. "All right," he agreed with a reluctant sigh. He'd deal with whatever was lurking around the perimeter of the cellar. He'd have to. He could hear Candy's teeth click as they began to chatter. She needed warmth. It was his responsibility to provide it. It was that simple.

"How's this?" Candy asked from a new position directly behind him. She had the flashlight aimed over his shoulder.

"Fine," Michael grumbled as he struggled to look competent. Okay, now this was a boiler. Its role in life was to boil. Somewhere there had to be a connection to a water source and some kind of valve he could turn to allow it into the system. Where?

"Oh!"

Michael swung his head around so fast he smacked it on a low pipe. "Ouch! What? What's wrong?"

Frantically Candy brushed the front of her robe with one hand. "One of those jumping cricket things landed right on me. It startled me, that's all."

"Man, you could have given me a heart attack. I thought you'd seen a rat or something." The little crickets

172 HOUSEMATES

were peanuts in his book. That scale, he could handle. He leaned back against the furnace and raised his arm, ready to lecture further. His hand knocked a lever. Running water. He heard water moving through pipes! Swinging around to stare at the boiler, he hit his head against the same low pipe.

"Damn it." But his heart wasn't in the curse. A hard twist to the lever he'd accidentally knocked increased the noise of moving fluids. "Hot damn!" he exulted. He had water in the boiler. Now all he needed was a method of heating it. He'd have Candy's body, if not her heart, warmed up in no time. He began studying the contours of the boiler with renewed interest. All that was required now was someplace to apply a match. Something that resembled a burner.

"Michael, hold still for a minute."

Uh-oh. "Why?"

"There's a spider on your back. Pretty big, too. I need to run upstairs for a tissue to pick it off with."

He could see it perfectly in his mind's eye. Eight legs, hairy and easily two inches in diameter. Michael closed his eyes briefly and held perfectly still. "Just knock it off now, will you?"

"With my bare hands?"

Black widows and tarantulas did not live this far north. He knew that. Sometimes, though, it was difficult for intellectual facts to overrule emotional reaction. "Smack it with the flashlight, then, or use the bottom of your slipper."

She objected to those ideas, too. "I'd hurt you."

"Just do it, okay? Just do it."

"Okay, but remember, you asked for it," she warned as she bashed him one on the back.

He barely noticed the pain, his relief was so great. When he opened his eyes again, there it was, right in front of him. "Aha!"

Candy jumped when he yelled and stumbled up against his back. Instant warmth. Instant cold when she carefully stepped back. Amazing.

"What? What have you got?"

"Gas. I've found the gas valve. Watch this." Damn, this was going to be good. Like a magician using a wand, Michael waved a match from the pack he'd brought downstairs. He lit it, turned the valve, then touched the flame to the pilot. "Ta-da!" he crowed as the spark gradually transferred across the surface of the burner. The smell of baking dust quickly permeated the air.

Michael felt like an all-conquering hero when Candy threw her arms around him.

"Michael, you're wonderful!"

"Yeah," he agreed immodestly. Nothing smelled sweeter, he decided, than the odor of heating dust and water. He wrapped his arms around her waist and hugged hard.

She laughed, reaching up to pull his head down, then kissed him, smack on the lips.

It was a most satisfactory end to a battle with a fire-breathing dragon, he decided as he kept one arm at her waist and guided her up the stairs. He'd have run a far more strenuous gauntlet than that to coax a smile out of Candy.

By the time they reached the first floor, some of the radiators had already begun to whistle like happy kettles. "Reminds me of my mother and her nightly cup of tea," Candy commented.

"Tea might warm us up while we wait for the heat to reach the second floor," Michael said, detouring toward the kitchen. It was crazy, but he felt a decidedly irrational

174 HOUSEMATES

stab of plain old jealousy. He didn't want Candy thinking of her mother. He was the one who was with her now, the one who'd battled the monster in the basement for her. He shook his head in exasperation. How could he be jealous of her *mother?* he asked himself as he plugged in the hot pot. He was losing it, no doubt about it.

His thinking was no better organized a short time later when he ushered Candy to the door of her bedroom. She gave him an odd look after the absent kiss he gave her, but he ignored it, pivoted on his heel and went to crawl into his lonely twin-size bed. He lay there, wide awake, flat on his back, both hands laced together behind his head and a pillow propping him up, stewing.

His actions lately puzzled him. Being around Candy brought out aspects of his personality he hadn't even known existed until a few months ago. He recognized he was conservative by nature. Heck, he'd always talked a good line about investing in old houses, even going so far as to look around a bit. But he'd never *done* anything about it. A month after meeting Candice Barr, his entire life's savings was in jeopardy.

He pulled his hands away and let his head sink into the pillow. And take this deal with Gary Felding over at Rust-safe. Never in his life had he interfered with another salesperson's calls. Definitely bad form. But look at the way he'd jumped with both feet into the middle of Candy's accounts. They weren't even partners, for heaven's sake. What must she think of him? He rolled his eyes. What must the rest of the office think of him?

Then there was the way he let her talk him into things.

Michael rubbed his nose in chagrin. Not only had he bought a patterned bed set for her, he'd gotten colors for himself, as well. Plain solids, to be sure, but definitely not white. Before you knew it, he'd be agreeing to the wallpaper she wanted for the kitchen and back hall.

HOUSEMATES

The room was heating up nicely, and the house was groaning its pleasure at being defrosted. He put his hands back behind his head and listened to the bed creak in Candy's room. It pleased him to hear her settling down at last. She could sleep thanks to the brilliant—if he did say so himself—duel he'd fought downstairs.

He studied the cracks in the ceiling. They were sufficiently large and the moonlight sufficiently bright that he could do that. Life, he decided was like that maze of interweaving trails up there. You could start down a certain path, but you never knew where you'd end up.

"The looney bin," he muttered as he determinedly closed his eyes and turned onto his side. "That's where I'll end up if Candy's got me comparing life to a cracked ceiling. I'm going to have to start watching it. There are definite symptoms of mental breakdown taking place here."

Then again, he thought as the bed squeaked once more in the other room, it wouldn't be a bad way to go if Candy was at his side.

His eyes opened wide as the thought registered. He'd been having a lot of peculiar thoughts like that lately. And Candy figured prominently in every single one of them.

"Well, what do you expect when the ghost of families past has tried everything but starting a war to push us together?" he asked himself. "It's ridiculous. An entire apartment building up in smoke. I mean, come on."

The most disgruntling aspect of the whole situation was that it looked like the only way he'd be allowed to take advantage of the situation would be to marry her. At least, he *assumed* he'd be allowed to take advantage of the situation at that point.

Restlessly he rolled on to his other side and stared at the dark shadows of a grouping of plastic crates he'd stacked open ends facing out so he could keep his clean folded clothes off the grungy floor.

This was what his life had come to. His clothes stuffed in baskets, him sleeping all alone while a gorgeous blonde slept in her solitary bed just down the hall. Eating meals cooked on a hot plate until the kitchen was remodeled. The pits. What's more, it was likely to remain the pits, probably until he cried uncle. Two in the morning was as good a time as any, he supposed. There was no percentage in fighting fate, he told himself as he flopped onto his stomach and wedged his pillow over his head. He would not have chosen marriage of his own free will, but evidently, what he had here was a case of *que sera* was going to darn well *sera*.

Heaven had pushed all the trappings of marriage on them, so he guessed they might as well legalize things before the neighbors began to talk. As far as he was concerned, the decision had been taken out of his hands. You can't fight city hall, and it looked as if you had even less chance against the ghostly equivalent. Besides, he'd be blameless. If—when—things fell apart, he would be absolutely in the clear.

His eyes began to drift shut. All he had to do now was let Candy know he was willing to bow to Upper Management. He just hoped he wasn't too late. Something told him she'd be less receptive than he might wish. When he'd come in, there'd been a pyramid of white paint cans downstairs. Candy must have picked them up on her way home. It bothered him more than he liked to admit that she had perhaps decided to listen to him. Now the idea of white walls struck him as sterile. He wanted the old Candy back. The one brimming with enthusiasm for this old wreck and full of off-the-wall decorating ideas. He wanted her to nest here. With him. After all, *que sera, sera*.

Candy rolled out of bed so abruptly the next morning she landed on the floor. "My God, what's happening?"

HOUSEMATES

she shrieked as another loud explosion reverberated from the basement. Hastily she disentangled herself from the sheets. She ignored her bruised hip. "Michael, wake up. We've got to get out of here. The house is going to blow up!"

When she reached the hall, Michael was coming out of his room. As if the house taking on a life of its own was not enough, now she had to deal with Michael in jeans and nothing else. She hoped her heart was up to the additional stress. Damn his hairy chest, anyway. "Michael," she cried as she hurried toward him. "What's going on?"

He waited on the top step, one hand on the banister. "I don't know. I was just going down to check. Something to do with the boiler, judging by the way all the pipes are shaking."

Candy clenched his arm with both of her hands when she reached him. "It's the gas we turned on, I know it. We've got to get out of here," she insisted, wide-eyed.

Michael covered her hands with one of his and considered the idea, then discarded it. "Nah. If it was gas, we'd already be blown to bits. This sounds almost like an air hammer. You stay here. I'll be right back."

"No. Listen, this is stupid. Let's get out of here and we'll just call somebody to come. Let them get blown up."

He shrugged. "Hey, whoever they are, they'll belong to *somebody* who'll be upset if we blow him or her to kingdom come."

"But not to me," she replied quickly. "And it's their job to know if that sound is harmless or not," she said, justifying her selfishness.

Michael felt a flash of elation. She cared. She was worried about his safety. He might be able to talk her into returning all the white paint, after all. But first things first. "I just want to take a peek and make sure it's not some-

178 HOUSEMATES

thing really obvious that will make us look stupid for falling apart."

"Then I'm coming with you." She sidled closer as another loud boom echoed up.

He put his arm around her. It would be very easy to pull her even closer, to start kissing her and make love to her right there. If the house exploded around them, it would only be apropos. Besides, with Candy in his arms he wasn't sure if he'd even notice.

Instead, he sighed. The house was turning into a bad joke, but it was all they'd have if they got married. "Let me run down real quick and take a look. I'll be right back."

Candy hovered at the top of the basement stairwell while Michael cautiously crept down and approached the boiler. After studying it a few minutes, he was back up. "It's the pipes," he informed her. "They're clanging like a son of a gun every time the boiler switches on. I must have flooded the system last night. Dress warm. I've shut the thing off until I can figure it out." Michael stood by the basement door and looked down at Candy. He made his decision. "It's early, though. We don't have to be at work for a while and we need to talk."

Candy's eyes widened. "About what?" she asked cautiously.

He shrugged in feigned nonchalance. "You. Me. This house. Us."

She searched his face and nodded once. "Right. The house. Us." Taking a fortifying breath, she turned toward the stairs. "I'll be right back." But as she passed by the little telephone stand in the hall, the phone rang. "Hello?"

"Who's calling at this time of the morning?" Michael hissed.

HOUSEMATES 179

Candy covered the mouthpiece with one hand and whispered, "It's Mary Frank. All excited." She listened a bit longer. "Thinks she's got a buyer."

"A buyer?" What was this?

"Some guy who saw the house before we did. Uh, thought it would be too much work. Couldn't find anything else in a neighborhood even half as good. Uh-huh, uh-huh, getting desperate, wife and kids still stuck out on the West Coast until he finds something, willing to pay us everything we put into the place, plus another ten thou."

Thunderstruck, Michael stared at her. "You're kidding."

"No," she whispered back, hand still over the mouthpiece. "Mary thinks the guy is dead serious." She removed her hand. "Yes. Yes, I heard everything you said, Mary. I'm still here. It's just kind of hard to take in."

"You can say that again."

"Shh. What did you say, Mary? Eight o'clock? This morning? The guy's nuts. No way is he coming through here at eight o'clock. I don't care how desperate he is. No, listen, Mary, Michael was trying to put in a new medicine cabinet into the bathroom wall for me last week, but he's only so strong, you know? It slipped in his hands just a bit and, bam, next thing you know, a corner of it came right through into the master bedroom. I haven't quite figured out how to repair a hole that size yet, so it's still there. And I hate to admit it, but I was trying to put together one of those little round wooden tables with the three legs that you're supposed to cover with a floor-length piece of fabric to hide how cheap-looking it is, you know the kind?" Candy took a breath.

"Yes, well, I thought if I put in some screws, it would make it stronger. Only, I didn't want the tops of the screws to show through the tablecloth, so I turned it upside down and screwed them in from underneath. Well, to make a

180 HOUSEMATES

long story even longer, I guess the screws I used were too long and I screwed the table to the floor. I was so mad at myself, and I really didn't want to see the damage to the floor, that— Basically, I guess what I'm telling you is that there's an upside-down table screwed to the floor in the middle of my bedroom.''

This time Michael took a breath for her. Amazing. And truthfully, he needed the oxygen himself. Everything that had seemed so clear in the middle of the night, the decisions he'd reached, all of it had just been invalidated. He wasn't trapped here in this money-eating pit. He could rejoin the world, send his sister some cash, get a nice apartment again. My God, he could come out of this smelling like a rose. He could make five thousand dollars in a couple of months. *He didn't have to get married.*

"Okay, okay. I'll see what I can do. But nine at the absolute earliest, you tell him, and not a minute before. Yes, I know. Right. I'm hanging up now, Mary. There's a lot to do here. Goodbye.''

Candy replaced the receiver with a sense of relief. "Michael, our little talk will have to wait, I'm afraid. We've got to get dressed and clean things up as best we can. Do you remember what happened to the screwdriver? I'm going to get that table off the floor first thing.'' She eyed the surrounding walls critically. "Too bad we didn't get the walls in here painted. This tarnished gold is depressing. Oh, well, I—''

"Candy,'' Michael interrupted, "I'm going to go for a run. I need to clear my head.'' And that was God's truth. His brain felt as though a cyclone had just passed through it. He needed to be by himself for a while, sort through the rubble, which was all that was left in his skull.

"A run! Michael, there's no time to—''

HOUSEMATES

"I'm sorry, but I really need to think something out. Besides, this guy saw the place in its original state. You've forgotten how bad that was. This'll look good to him."

"I don't know, Michael. At least if I could find a picture or something to hang over that hole in the master bedroom, I'd feel better."

"Check the attic," Michael advised, taking the steps two at a time in his rush to change into jogging attire. He really needed to get out of the house. "There's still a bunch of stuff up there we haven't gotten to yet." He was out the door less than five minutes later.

Michael ran until his lungs ached. Only then did he realize how hard he'd been pushing. "Slow down," he advised himself. "No point in having a heart attack at this point in the ball game. Not when things are finally looking up." The problem was, he decided as he forcibly slowed his pace, he'd had so many emotional punches thrown at him lately, he was getting slaphappy. He wasn't sure things *were* looking up.

He'd been running straight east down Lake Avenue. It was a pretty, tree-lined boulevard with large older homes that had aged graciously. It also dead-ended right at the village of Wilmette's public beach. Michael entered the park. Before him, Lake Michigan shivered in the early-morning autumn chill. He slowed further and tried to absorb some of the serenity of the scene before him.

"What this basically boils down to," he announced to the amazingly blue body of water, "is that if this guy comes through with an offer, I'm off the hook. I should be happy. Ecstatic even. Instead, I feel like strangling the jerk for upsetting the applecart."

He stood stock-still and stared at the rolling waves. Finally he began to feel the bite of the wind. "Now, why is that? I'll tell you why. I want Candy! If we get out of this

182   HOUSEMATES

mess before I've got her, my chances are zero, zilch, nada!''

He turned to begin pacing along the shore and promptly tripped over a piece of half-buried driftwood. He found himself on all fours, one hand firmly planted on a dead alewife. Raising his head heavenward, he wailed, "You didn't let me finish. I want her that way, but I want her a lot of other ways, too." And it was true, he realized as he picked himself up and brushed the sand off his hands and knees. That was why when he'd finally decided fate had him boxed in last night and he wouldn't escape without offering marriage, he'd felt relief, instead of anger.

Now he had to decide by himself. Whatever spirit in that house had knocked him over the head several times to get his attention now appeared to be backing off—probably just to give the two of them the illusion they had some say in all this.

"The answer's yes!" he yelled skyward. "Yes, do you hear? To heck with my parents, my grandparents, *and* my sister. I'm different. I *will* make this work because I badly *want* it to work."

Suddenly he realized how cold he'd become and he quickened his pace, moving from a walk into a slow jog. He didn't go directly back to the house but, instead, ran around the village a bit, watching it wake up. It was a nice little town, even if it did shriek *suburbia*. "I'm going to love living here. Candy will, too. Our children will love it, wait and see. In fact, I think I'll take Candy out after work to look at station wagons."

The bells in the church tower two blocks down from the house chimed eight o'clock as he went by, and Michael turned on more speed when he should have been slowing for a cool-down. He needed to get back to Candy.

Candy was coming down the walk from the front door as Michael approached the house. He knew the moment

HOUSEMATES

she saw him. Her hands flew to her hips and the worried look left her face to be replaced by one of irritation.

"Darn it, Michael, where have you been? I was just coming out to search for you. I found a picture to hang over the hole in the wall up here, nothing great, but it'll have to do. And I managed to unscrew the table from the floor, but could you at least come collect some of your tools and get them out of sight? Oh, and make your bed, okay? You know, you've got a lot at stake here, too. The least you could do is pitch in a little."

"Candy, listen to me," he said urgently. "Call Mary and cancel. We're not selling. We're staying here. You and I."

Dead silence met his decree. Easily thirty seconds passed. "I beg your pardon?" she finally asked.

"You heard me. We're going to fix this place up, but for us. You can buy all the wallpaper you want," he offered generously, "so long as it's cheap. I'll even help you hang the stuff." And if that wasn't a magnanimous romantic offer, he didn't know what was.

"Oh, no. Any wallpapering that gets done around here, I'll do." She quickly turned down his offer, remembering his lack of finesse with a mop and shuddering at the thought of replacing it with a wallpaper-paste brush. Then she realized she'd focused on a piddling detail when something far more significant was maybe taking place.

She didn't want to embarrass herself by asking point-blank, just in case she was wrong, but there was the barest possibility that Michael, in his ever romantic, suave manner, might have just proposed. It would be nice to know for sure. She'd come to the conclusion the night of that infamous World Series game that she could be talked into trashing her life's schedule for Michael. She'd realized that night she loved him, and love could not be put on a schedule. She'd even decided a December red-and-white wedding might not be too terribly tacky. What it boiled down

184 HOUSEMATES

to was if Michael was actually proposing here, she'd accept in less time than it took to flick on her computer. She just needed to know precisely what he had in mind and that his commitment would be as firm and strong as hers.

"Michael, exactly what are you saying?" she asked as the last of the season's maple leaves drifted down around them. "I have to warn you, I'm not interested in some kind of cheap open-ended affair."

Michael held up his hands in a protestation of innocence. "Shh, not so loud. The house might hear." Obviously he hadn't made himself clear. "Candy, we couldn't carry off a cheap open-ended affair if we wanted to. We tried, remember? I'm talking marriage here, with all the loose ends tied up in a nice legal bow."

"If this is a proposal, it's the most unromantic one I've ever had."

His eyes narrowed. "How many have you had?"

"None of your business."

Unromantic, huh? She rated them? Well, he'd give her something worth scoring a few points. Right there on the front sidewalk, at eight o'clock in the morning, his sweats sticking to him and dead brown leaves swirling around him, Michael dropped to his knees in front of her.

"Candy, my delicious little morsel, I love you. If, as you search the recesses of your heart, you can find even a crumb of affection for me, I beg you to put me out of my misery. Marry me and I'll give you a daughter we'll name Sugar. Easter Sundays we'll dress her in hats with ribbons, fake flowers and elastic chin straps, froufrou dresses and little socks with lace at the ankles. We'll all walk to church together. You, me, Sugar—oh, and our son, Raising." He shifted a bit as pebbles dug into his knees. She'd better say yes, and fast.

Candy waved weakly at the next-door neighbor who'd come out in her bathrobe to retrieve the morning paper.

The woman stared at Michael as she walked down her driveway then all the way back up. Michael didn't so much as blink. Candy wrinkled her nose at him. "Raising Cane? That's pathetic."

Michael shrugged a shoulder negligently. "If he puts half as many baseballs through windows as I did, he'll live up to it," he explained.

"We'll name him Matthew," she informed him firmly. "And a girl will be Beth Ann."

"Is that a yes?"

"It's a maybe. I intend my marriage vows to be forever. If you're not thinking in those terms, I want to know now."

Michael held up his right hand. "I am, Candy. I swear. You'll never get rid of me." He made a solemn cross on his chest over the general vicinity of his heart. "Can you say yes now? If I promise I will do everything in my power to make you love being Candy Cane, can I get up? My knees are killing me."

The window curtain next door twitched. Candy noticed it out of the corner of her eye as she studied the man before her. "Michael, you're an idiot."

"But a lovable one?"

Her eyes filled and she sniffed a bit. "Yeah, a lovable one. And I do. Love you, that is."

"And you'll marry me and stay with me forever and ever?"

"Yeah. Forever and ever."

"All right!" Michael leapt to his feet, exultant. He swept Candy into his arms and carried her up the walk and stopped in front of the door. "Turn the knob," he instructed, "and push it open. I'm going to carry you over the threshold."

"Don't you want to wait till we're married?" she asked as she followed directions and opened the door with one hand. Her other arm she left wrapped around his neck.

He put one foot up on the sill and paused, wanting her to understand. "No. This is it, Candy. This is our beginning as a committed couple. There'll be no going back now. We're going to call Mary Frank and then we're going to put that pyramid of white paint you built in the hall into the car and take it back. We'll have it tinted any color you want. Then I'm going to buy a power sprayer and cover these walls with color. Just for you. By the time I'm done, there won't be a speck of white anywhere in the place."

Candy laughed and sniffed again as Michael carried her into their home. "Purple. Will you paint the walls purple for me?"

"Uh, purple? I tell you what, let's discuss it in the car when we go to the paint store. I'm sure we can reach a compromise we can both live with."

You know what? So was she. "Go take a shower, Michael. I'll be waiting for you when you come out."

He studied her long and hard and knew she spoke the truth. She'd committed. "Thank God," he breathed, and leaned down to kiss her. Nothing fell on them. Nothing smoked. The floor remained under their feet. He was on a roll. "After we drop off the paint," he told her when they'd both recovered a bit from the kiss, "we'll stop by the hardware store. Get some extra slats for the bed in the master bedroom. We may break a few tonight."

Over the course of their life together, they broke several, but found they made great kindling for the fireplace, which worked like a charm once the chimney had been cleared.

"Michael?"

HOUSEMATES

"Hmm?"

"Are you ready for numbers one, two and three to show up in seven months' time?"

"What? No, tell me you're kidding, please. I married you, didn't I? I behaved. Surely the house wouldn't inflict triplets on us! I know it's waited a long while for a family to move in, but triplets? Dear Lord."

"Just kidding. I only did that to make twins sound better."

There was momentary dead silence. "Twins? We're having twins?"

"Yeah, I found out this afternoon."

He thought about that, then answered cautiously, "That's okay, I guess. Just two. You know what? We're getting off damn light. Take that, house!" he yelled. "There're only two!"

There was no response, but three years later, another duo arrived and two years after that...

*   *   *   *   *

HE'S MORE THAN A MAN, HE'S ONE OF OUR

DANIEL'S DADDY
Stella Bagwell

Jess Malone didn't want to raise his son, Daniel, alone, but he didn't want to get married, either. He'd already learned that loving a woman didn't mean she'd stay. But Jess couldn't deny his son a mother. And Daniel had his heart set on Hannah Dunbar. Now all Jess had to do was make Hannah his wife—without losing *his* heart....

Look for *DANIEL'S DADDY* by Stella Bagwell. Available in July.

Fall in love with our FABULOUS FATHERS!

Take 4 bestselling love stories FREE

Plus get a FREE surprise gift!

Special Limited-time Offer

Mail to Silhouette Reader Service™

**3010 Walden Avenue
P.O. Box 1867
Buffalo, N.Y. 14269-1867**

YES! Please send me 4 free Silhouette Romance™ novels and my free surprise gift. Then send me 6 brand-new novels every month, which I will receive months before they appear in bookstores. Bill me at the low price of $2.19 each plus 25¢ delivery and applicable sales tax, if any.* That's the complete price and—compared to the cover prices of $2.75 each—quite a bargain! I understand that accepting the books and gift places me under no obligation ever to buy any books. I can always return a shipment and cancel at any time. Even if I never buy another book from Silhouette, the 4 free books and the surprise gift are mine to keep forever.

215 BPA ANRP

Name	(PLEASE PRINT)	
Address		Apt. No.
City	State	Zip

This offer is limited to one order per household and not valid to present Silhouette Romance™ subscribers. *Terms and prices are subject to change without notice. Sales tax applicable in N.Y.

USROM-94R   ©1990 Harlequin Enterprises Limited

It's our 1000th Silhouette Romance, and we're celebrating!

Join us for a special collection of love stories by authors you've loved for years, and new favorites you've just discovered. Join the celebration...

April
REGAN'S PRIDE by **Diana Palmer**
MARRY ME AGAIN by **Suzanne Carey**

May
THE BEST IS YET TO BE by **Tracy Sinclair**
CAUTION: BABY AHEAD by **Marie Ferrarella**

June
THE BACHELOR PRINCE by **Debbie Macomber**
A ROGUE'S HEART by **Laurie Paige**

July
IMPROMPTU BRIDE by **Annette Broadrick**
THE FORGOTTEN HUSBAND by **Elizabeth August**

Silhouette Romance...vibrant, fun and emotionally rich! Take another look at us! And as part of the celebration, readers can receive a FREE gift!

You'll fall in love all over again with Silhouette Romance!

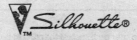

CEL1000

It's our 1000th Silhouette Romance™, and we're celebrating!

And to say "THANK YOU" to our wonderful readers, we would like to send you a

FREE AUSTRIAN CRYSTAL BRACELET

This special bracelet truly captures the spirit of CELEBRATION 1000! and is a stunning complement to any outfit! And it can be yours FREE just for enjoying SILHOUETTE ROMANCE™.

FREE GIFT OFFER

To receive your free gift, complete the certificate according to directions. Be certain to enclose the required number of proofs-of-purchase. Requests must be received no later than August 31, 1994. Please allow 6 to 8 weeks for receipt of order. Offer good while quantities of gifts last. Offer good in U.S. and Canada only.

And that's not all! Readers can also enter our...

CELEBRATION 1000! SWEEPSTAKES

In honor of our 1000th SILHOUETTE ROMANCE™, we'd like to award $1000 to a lucky reader!

As an added value every time you send in a completed offer certificate with the correct amount of proofs-of-purchase, your name will automatically be entered in our CELEBRATION 1000! Sweepstakes. The sweepstakes features a grand prize of $1000. PLUS, 1000 runner-up prizes of a FREE SILHOUETTE ROMANCE™, autographed by one of CELEBRATION 1000!'s special featured authors will be awarded. These volumes are sure to be cherished for years to come, a true commemorative keepsake.

DON'T MISS YOUR OPPORTUNITY TO WIN! ENTER NOW!

CELOFFER

CELEBRATION 1000! FREE GIFT OFFER

ORDER INFORMATION:

To receive your free AUSTRIAN CRYSTAL BRACELET, send three original proof-of-purchase coupons from any SILHOUETTE ROMANCE™ title published in April through July 1994 with the Free Gift Certificate completed, plus $1.75 for postage and handling (check or money order—please do not send cash) payable to Silhouette Books CELEBRATION 1000! Offer. Hurry! Quantities are limited.

FREE GIFT CERTIFICATE   096 KBM

Name:_____

Address:_____

City:_____ State/Prov.:_____ Zip/Postal:_____

Mail this certificate, three proofs-of-purchase and check or money order to CELEBRATION 1000! Offer, Silhouette Books, 3010 Walden Avenue, P.O. Box 9057, Buffalo, NY 14269-9057 or P.O. Box 622, Fort Erie, Ontario L2A 5X3. Please allow 4-6 weeks for delivery. Offer expires August 31, 1994.

PLUS

Every time you submit a completed certificate with the correct number of proofs-of-purchase, you are automatically entered in our CELEBRATION 1000! SWEEPSTAKES to win the GRAND PRIZE of $1000 CASH! PLUS, 1000 runner-up prizes of a FREE Silhouette Romance™, autographed by one of CELEBRATION 1000!'s special featured authors, will be awarded. No purchase or obligation necessary to enter. See below for alternate means of entry and how to obtain complete sweepstakes rules.

CELEBRATION 1000! SWEEPSTAKES
NO PURCHASE OR OBLIGATION NECESSARY TO ENTER

You may enter the sweepstakes without taking advantage of the CELEBRATION 1000! FREE GIFT OFFER by hand-printing on a 3" x 5" card (mechanical reproductions are not acceptable) your name and address and mailing it to: CELEBRATION 1000! Sweepstakes, P.O. Box 9057, Buffalo, NY 14269-9057 or P.O. Box 622, Fort Erie, Ontario L2A 5X3. Limit: one entry per envelope. Entries must be sent via First Class mail and be received no later than August 31, 1994. No liability is assumed for lost, late or misdirected mail.

Sweepstakes is open to residents of the U.S. (except Puerto Rico) and Canada, 18 years of age or older. All federal, state, provincial, municipal and local laws apply. Offer void wherever prohibited by law. Odds of winning dependent on the number of entries received. For complete rules, send a self-addressed, stamped envelope to: CELEBRATION 1000! Rules, P.O. Box 4200, Blair, NE 68009.

 ONE PROOF OF PURCHASE

096KBM

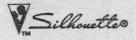